CAPTAIN
KIDD

BOOKS BY JEROME CHARYN

NOVELS

NONFICTION

CAPTAIN KIDD

JEROME CHARYN

ST. MARTIN'S PRESS NEW YORK

THOMAS DUNNE BOOKS.
An imprint of St. Martin's Press.

Book design by Jane Adele Regina

Library of Congress Cataloging-in-Publication Data
Charyn, Jerome.
  Captain Kidd / Jerome Charyn.
    p. cm.
  "Thomas Dunne books."
  ISBN 0-312-20506-6 (hardcover)
  1. World War, 1939–1945 Fiction. 2. Patton, George S. (George Smith), 1888–1945 Fiction. I. Title.
PS3553.H33C37 1999
813'.54—dc21   99-21747
                                               CIP

First Edition: June 1999

10   9   8   7   6   5   4   3   2   1

CAPTAIN KIDD

ROLAND

1

● We were hunting treasure. It was simple as that. We shot at Germans when we had to, but it was only an accident of war, as the Old Man would say. We weren't rear-echelon jokers who came into a kill zone after the fighting was over and looked for loot. We were always far ahead of the Old Man and his tanks. I was the youngest captain in our show, a kid out of college. But the Old Man took a liking to me. I was his court jester, his scribe, his philosophical companion. I kept his dog company when the Old Man was on some kind of tactical alert. I took Willie out for long walks, watched him piss all over the terrain. He was a ferocious bull terrier who was capable of biting off your kneecap. Willie didn't like me. He only cared about the Old Man. But he was the best damn blinder in the world. I could go anywhere with General Patton's dog in my jeep. Who would have stopped me? Captain Roland P. Kahn, with his squad of colored MPs. It was one of my obligations to select the Old Man's corps of body-guards. I picked the colored MPs. But the truth is, those military policemen picked me.

I'd gone to Cornell, where my dad had also gone and

endowed a couple of chairs in my mother's name. He was an investment banker who'd inherited my grandfather's fortune. My mother's people, the Karps, had built the first department store in America. They were like pirates, swallowing up other companies, other stores. The colored MPs didn't know much about my background, but they still called me Captain Kidd. They might have laughed at their own acumen if they'd discovered all the pirates in my family tree.

I was a pirate, and I'm not sure why. I was scheduled to marry a girl who was at least as rich as mom. I'd graduated magna cum laude, had a Phi Beta Kappa key, was a perfect candidate for Harvard Law. I had the world's own tit in my mouth. I'd studied art and banking, was as sturdy as one of the Old Man's tanks. And I decided to steal.

I could have been court-martialed, hanged from a tree, or murdered by my chief rival, Romulus Rivers, a supply sergeant. Rom had a big advantage over me. He had trucks and his own depot, where he could hide the loot. But he didn't have General Patton's dog, and he couldn't forage in the front lines. His team could only wait and descend like jackals.

"Jewboy," he said, "I'll bet the Old Man's dog is part kike."

"Sergeant, stand at attention when you're talking to me."

"Yes, sir," he said, whipping the blade of his hand into a mock salute. "I'm gonna snitch on you, Cap, gonna tell the Old Man."

"Wonderful. I'll do all the paperwork."

"Don't need your paperwork. I'll just recite about all the cognac you took and all the gold bars, how you and your niggers broke into heinie warehouses and took and took and took."

"We didn't have to break in, Rom. The heinies left behind whatever they couldn't carry. And you know my policy. I never touch gold. That goes right into the Third Army's vault."

"But you must have a million dollars in merchandise."

"Don't bark at me, Rom, and don't threaten."

"Then I'll kill you, kill you with my own hands."

"Fine," I said, "as long as you salute me first."

I went back to my jeep, where Willie was waiting with one of my MPs, Sergeant Booker Bell. He was looking very serious. I never pulled rank on Booker Bell. He'd saved my ass a thousand times. I was a pathetic soldier without him, could barely clean my pearl-handled Colt, a gift from the Old Man.

Willie growled after I jumped into the driver's seat. He sat up front with me on a special pillow, Booker behind us, smoking Cuban cigars from our private cache. He blew a magnificent ring in Romulus' direction. "We're gonna have to hurt that man, hurt him bad."

"He's harmless," I said.

"That is dumb, really dumb. The man has a big mouth. And he don't trade in trinkets, like us. He's lifting bars of gold he can't even sell, because he doesn't have our connections."

"Booker," I said, "I'm not making war on a United States supply sergeant."

"Where'd you grow up? In a silver cradle? He's our enemy. The Germans are just fanatics and fools."

"Tell that to the Old Man."

"He'd agree. . . . Who the hell have we been catching in the forests, huh? Women and children, Hitler's Boy Scouts."

"Boy Scouts with burp guns," I said.

"Go on," Booker said. "I'm disgusted with you. Drive us home, Captain Kidd."

We never had a problem at the checkpoints. The password was "Betty Grable," but the guards would simply salute us when they saw Willie on his pillow. They just assumed that Booker Bell was one more anomaly in the ETO, some military strategist, a black wizard on the Old Man's staff.

I didn't care what the wizard said. There were German commandos running around in American uniforms, trying to capture the Old Man. It was a desperate trick. But I was responsible for the Old Man's safety. And if we caught a GI on the road who couldn't recite "Betty Grable" or one of George Raft's films, I was prepared to shoot him with my uncleaned Colt.

There were a couple of Red Cross doughnut girls outside the Old Man's trailer. Willie adored the doughnut girls, who fed him black coffee and little chocolate pies. He slobbered around the tall, beautiful one with red hair. She was from Minneapolis, and her name was Margaret Young. It was her second month in the ETO. She'd left Wellesley College to come and live in a German forest. I was crazy about her, slept with her as often as I could. Margaret knew about my fiancée. But it was wartime, and any future marriage was miles and miles away. I was dying to write Lizabeth Rose, tell her that our engagement was off, but Margaret wouldn't sleep with me if I dropped my "honey" back home.

I kissed her before I went in to see the Old Man, kissed her as hard as I could, while Willie was slobbering.

"Do we get the truck tonight?" I asked like a schoolboy. "Is it our turn?"

"That depends on how many doughnuts we give out. But I'll finagle," she said.

"You can give whatever you have left to Willie."

"That's immoral, dumping doughnuts on a dog."

"You're too clever, all you Wellesley girls, studying Shakespeare when I have to make do with our pathetic little lending library."

"Shut up, Roland," she said. "The general wants you. He's lonesome for Willie."

I kept thinking of her red hair. I brought Willie into the trailer. The Old Man didn't have any secrets from me. He'd shout at Willie in public, put up a big front, a three-star general reprimanding his dog, but he danced around in his boots, tugged at Willie's tail, and gurgled like a baby. "Little man miss his papa, huh?"

The goddamn dog loved every minute of it. I could have been invisible. But when I started to tiptoe out the door, the Old Man said, "Stay, Rollie . . . I'm hopeless without that pup."

He had the blue eyes of a conqueror. I was almost as tall

as the general, six one and a half, but I didn't have that lightning look of a man who was moving tanks inside his head. I worshipped him, even with his faults. I could surround him with colored MPs, but he said that his colored troops weren't natural fighters, like the Hun. And he'd remind me of all the "Jewy Jewesses" he'd met at cocktail parties in London.

"Ever been inside a synagogue, Rollie?"

"No, sir."

His brows knit while he rubbed noses with Willie. "Then how does a son of a bitch like you talk to God?"

"It's difficult, sir."

"Rollie," he said, "I won't have an atheist on my staff. Do you believe in God, or not?"

I lied to the Old Man. "Of course I believe . . . sir."

"Then how do you talk to Him, how do you pray?"

"Before I go to bed, sir."

"Every night?"

I was still thinking of Margaret's red hair. "Almost, sir."

"Son," he said, "you're a mighty big bullshitter."

He put on his battle jacket, his silk scarf, his pearl-handled guns, the helmet that hugged his head. He winked at Willie. "Do I look like Flash Gordon, or the Man from Mars?"

The press corps loved the Old Man, would constantly find nicknames for him. They couldn't get enough of George. They'd rather scribble about him than the nabobs at SHAEF. He was their own fighting general. He didn't talk about redesigning Europe; he talked attack. Topside wanted him to deliver canned speeches to all the columnists. Topside was afraid of his fury, tried to muzzle him. Topside didn't want any more incidents with George. He'd slapped a soldier who complained of battle fatigue. He'd rant about niggers and kikes, but Topside needed George. He was winning the war. George had sliced Germany in half, his tanks had made their lightning runs, and he was routing German battalions that rode to war on bicycles. We had fifty German and Hungarian generals in PW cages. But I wouldn't let the Old Man deliver speeches that Topside wanted him to deliver. He had a thin, raspy voice that could only come alive with anger or play. And I had to rehearse George, sting him a little before we marched into the big tent.

"Rollie," he moaned, "I'll put my foot in my mouth. I always do. . . . The sons of bitches won't let me take Berlin. Ike says we have to wait for the Russkies. I'm a winning general, and I can't win."

"But you won't mention Ike," I said, "and you won't mention Berlin, or Jewy Jewesses, or the superiority of the white race."

"Then you meet with the press, not me," the Old Man said, with a trigger in his blue eyes.

"Georgie," I said.

It always angered the Old Man when I talked to him like he talked to Willie.

"Rollie, I'll demote you. You're a runt."

"I'm as tall as you are, Georgie, and I'm wearing one of your guns. You'll go out there with Willie, slap him on the rump, and you'll have reporters eating out of your hand."

"But what will I say?"

"Tell them about the elephants. . . . That'll warm them up."

The Old Man shivered, but I wasn't worried. I led him and Willie out of the trailer, and we were like a little song-and-dance team when we arrived at his war tent. It was packed. The Old Man whispered in my ear. "Look at me. I'll never have a natural-born fighting face."

"Your face is fine," I said, and maneuvered him to the platform, Willie at his heels. Margaret was inside the tent with the other doughnut girls. The columnists kept staring at her, and eating their pencils with envy. They couldn't get near Red. She wouldn't even give them one little dance. I was her soldier. The columnists called me Herr Goebbels, because I had my own diabolic influence on George. But they never mentioned me in their dispatches. They didn't dare. They were frightened of what Uncle Henry might do. Henry Morgenthau, secretary of the treasury, wasn't really my uncle. But he was a friend of my father's, and I'd been to the White House with Uncle Henry before the war.

I couldn't take my eyes off Margaret. I was as stupid and ferocious as the Old Man's white pup. "Red, I love you, Red."

She smiled at me. "Go upstairs with your general."

I hopped onto the platform, stood with Willie. The Old Man wouldn't begin without me. I was his kindhearted censor.

"Ladies and gentlemen," he shouted. His voice wasn't

raspy or thin. "Am I the Man from Mars, or the Green Hornet?"

The whole tent clapped. The Old Man was treating the press conference like a bit of tactical warfare.

"The elephant should have conquered the planet, not us. He's stronger, but God only gave him one trunk. With two trunks he would have developed our dexterity, our suppleness of mind, and *he'd* be chasing Hitler . . ."

The reporters laughed. I looked at Red. I was in love.

I didn't dance with her that night. We had dinner with the general. He was crazy about her too, but his craziness wasn't as specific as mine. He invited all the doughnut girls. We drank white wine that I had stolen from one of the warehouses and put into the general's private stock. I was a very loyal thief. The Old Man ate simply in the field, and he'd share whatever he had with his soldiers. I wouldn't let any of the columnists near our dinner table. The Old Man would have had to perform, and they would have ogled Red.

"We must not die gallantly," he would have said. "We must devastate, kill like greedy angels." I didn't want to hear that. We didn't talk shop. He was very gallant with the girls. But his blue eyes would glaze over, and it wasn't about liebfraumilch. He couldn't stop dreaming war. Strategies would come to him in the middle of a conversation. His brain would explode for a minute, and then he'd be there with us again, ask about a girl's mother, father, or beau. But he was delicate with Red. He didn't ask her any questions. He fed

Willie from his own plate, and we sang songs that had nothing to do with Hitler and the war, while Willie slobbered and stared at Red with his pink eyes.

I couldn't eat. I wanted to live with Red inside her doughnut truck, day and night. I'd lose her once the war ended. But I couldn't tell the Old Man that he was capturing German generals at too fast a rate. "We have to hit the Hun between the eyes," he'd say. Meanwhile, I bartered in liebfraumilch and sparkling wine and made my associates a little rich.

I didn't take wine or chocolate back to the doughnut truck. We had our own pillow, blankets, and a mattress that Red kept for GIs who got dizzy between patrols. I borrowed one of the Old Man's big flashlights and a pack of cards. Red loved to play casino. She always won. I'd undress her during a game, forget about the bundles I had to build.

No one bothered Captain Kidd. We closed the curtains in the truck's little window. Her freckles excited me, the perfume of her armpits, flesh like wild strawberries that you couldn't find anywhere in the German winter. I began to have lightning thoughts like the Old Man, my mind ripping into Red's future, wondering where she'd be after the Russkies took Berlin.

"Will you go back to school, Red?"

"Don't spoil it. . . . I love you, Captain Kidd. Isn't that enough?"

"But we could . . ."

There was a little tap on the door.

"Son of a bitch," I said, "is that the midnight watch? I'm

not a heinie. I'm Captain Roland P. Kahn. The password is 'Betty Grable.' I can tell—"

"Rollie, come out of there."

I recognized the voice. It was an officer from G-2, the Old Man's intelligence team. Lieutenant Gabriel. I'd give him bottles of cognac from time to time. It wasn't a bribe. I liked Gabe. We'd come from the same fraternity at Cornell.

I put on my coat and climbed down from the truck.

"Better be good, Gabe. I was proposing to Red, asking her to become a spinster for me."

"While you marry money?"

"I'm a Kahn. We don't marry money. We firm up our positions, we triangulate . . . what do you want?"

"Nothing, Rollie. Some advice. Distance yourself from Sergeant Rivers. I hear G-5 is gonna arrest him tomorrow for trafficking in gold. And he has your name in his little black book."

"I never touch gold."

"Rollie, it will break the Old Man's heart. . . . You have three choices: kiss Romulus' ass, destroy his black book, or destroy Romulus. Good night."

I climbed back into the truck. Red wasn't planning her future, with or without me. Red was all business, worrying about the ten of diamonds and the two of spades, the big and little casino.

There was another "bump, bump" on the door. I grabbed my pearl-handled Colt. It could have been Hitler. I would have shot his eyes out.

"Gabe," I shouted, "that you?"

Bump, bump.

I opened the door. It was Willie, banging the truck with his snout, his pink eyes on fire. I let him in. He lay down next to Margaret, curled between her legs, happy as a hornet that had stung everybody he had to sting and was coming home to mama. He growled at me.

"Shut up, Willie."

He listened to Red. She started to laugh as she raked in the ten of diamonds.

"Big casino," I muttered, my future slipping into the enormous bundle of cards that Red was building, like her own war tent.

2

• We were foraging, going out further than we should, Captain Kidd with Booker Bell and the pup. We sailed on muddy water in the general's own jeep. There was talk of a fabulous depot, filled with cognac and gold bars too big for a man to carry.

Booker was talking, but I watched the terrain. The ground began to dry, and suddenly we were in a magic forest.

"Are you listening to me, Captain Kidd? We have to smoke Romulus before the inspector general grabs his ass."

"Rom can write my name a million times in his black book. It doesn't prove a thing. We don't keep inventory. There's nothing on paper, not one sale."

"Dream on, little man. If Romulus goes down, we go down. That's called American arithmetic."

There was a curious missile ahead of us, at the side of the road. Somebody in the very long skirts of a Hungarian general was sitting on the stump of a tree. I was a good scout. I could spot a German or Hungarian general by the length and the color of his winter coat—and the shape of his ceremonial silver dagger. But this general could have been shoved, or shot, into the forest. He was the perfect scarecrow, a bag of bones. He didn't even try to flee from us, or surrender his dagger. He sat on the stump. Willie started to growl.

The general was wearing lipstick, had big brown eyes. He couldn't have been more than twelve years old. Booker and I didn't even have to guess. The kid belonged to some whorehouse for Hungarian generals. He didn't flirt. He looked at us with the sadness of a boy who'd lost all his bearings. He didn't have an internal compass, like Booker, Willie, and myself. I couldn't seem to return his gaze.

"Get into the wagon," I said, "*schnell.*"

He slid off his stump and got into the front of the jeep. I had to quiet Willie, keep him from biting the little general's nose off. I fed chocolate to the pup, while the boy watched Willie swallow. I was familiar with Willie's habits. He wouldn't let an intruder eat with him, so I had to drop half a chocolate bar into the general's pocket.

Had my doubts about this magic forest. It was like a movie set, put there to hide something. The forest cleared. We'd entered some kind of labor camp with its own little factory and a castle that sat on a hill. The castle annoyed me more than the camp. It was a little too picturesque.

Three Russian PWs were hanging from hooks on a wall. The spittle had frozen to their chins and formed crooked icicles. Their faces had turned completely blue. I left them there. I didn't have the heart to tamper with those hooks. We got down off the jeep with Willie and entered one of the buildings. I wasn't looking for cognac or bars of gold. I found a whole inventory of American uniforms, with our damn shoulder patch: a white A in a blue background, sitting inside a big red O. The American Army of Occupation. And I realized what this laager was all about. The camp was nothing but a cover for German commandos, training to capture *our* Green Hornet.

I wanted to interrogate the kid, but I couldn't arrest a twelve-year-old general, and his lipstick made me cautious. There was a skunk hiding in the laager, a family of skunks, and I had to find that family. But we didn't find a thing other than mouse droppings and more shoulder patches.

We never even searched the factory. It would have been useless. I looked up at the castle, wondering if some Lorelei would serenade us from the windows. But Loreleis didn't come to labor camps. They sat on rocks in the middle of the Rhine.

A rabbit of a man came down from the castle and introduced himself as the Baron von Braun. He glanced at my uniform, called me Herr Captain, and couldn't keep his eyes off the pup. He spoke better English than half the Third Army. He was wearing tattered clothes. The factory belonged to him, he said.

"Baron, what the hell does it produce?"

"Ball bearings. We ran out of spare parts. We've been idle since the summer."

"And you let your Russian prisoners sweep the floor."

"I can't help it, Herr Captain, if they send us all the scum, like this indignity." He pointed to the little general. "He lived in the officers' brothel, when we had officers. They ran away. He's a Gypsy, born in filth. Let me take him off your hands."

"Baron," I said, "your sovereignty is over. You're surrendering to us."

"Surrender? What for? I'm not a combatant."

"No. You're the emperor of a slave labor camp. . . . Now tell me about the uniforms?"

"What uniforms?"

I clutched his lapels, lifted him off the ground. He was kind of heavy for a rabbit. "You've been housing a team of assassins, Baron. Or maybe *commandos* is a kinder word. You supply them with uniforms, documents, and English sentences, I suppose. Did you tell them that Betty Grable was going steady with George Raft until she married Harry James?"

"I don't understand."

"Sure you do. Harry can play the horn, but he didn't grow up in Hell's Kitchen, like George. Did you see him and Cagney in *Each Dawn I Die*?"

"Herr Captain, I have a frozen castle and a sleeping factory. I'm not a Hollywood mogul."

I winked at Willie. "Baron, whose pup is that?"

"Everybody knows about Herr General Patton's bulldog."

"Little man," Booker said, "we have work to do. Ask the baron where he keeps his cognac and his caviar."

"Bookie, I'm not in a trading mood."

"Then arrest him, put him in our truck."

"Not a chance. If he sits with you, the commandos won't come near us. They'll smell a trap."

"Then what are we gonna do with the mother?"

18

"Gag him, tie him up."

"I protest," the baron said. "I'm a noncombatant."

We brought him into the laager, stuffed his mouth with rags, and tied him to a table with pieces of wire.

"Captain Kidd, we gonna do business or not?"

"The whole setup stinks. A laager with three dead Russians, a baron who comes down from the hill . . ."

"And a bunch of American uniforms. But if you're telling me this is a commandos' college, I don't believe it. We would have picked up other signs."

We went back to the jeep. Romulus was waiting for us with a burp gun. Willie growled at him.

"Shaddap, Willie. . . . Where's the gold?"

There was a demented look in Rom's eyes, as if some demon had let him out of a jar.

"I'll kill your nigger," he said. "I swear. And the dog. And you, Captain Kidd."

"Slow down, hillbilly," Booker said. "I eat rednecks, eat them alive."

Rom fired the burp gun between the humped toes of Booker's combat boots. "I ain't fooling," he said. "This is the heinies' main storage dump. This is where Hitler keeps his gold and waits for the world to end. . . . What's that kid doing here?"

"He's a general," I said.

Romulus started to laugh. "The heinies are sure hard up. Why's he wearing lipstick?"

"Shame on you, Rom," Booker said. "Ain't you ever met the mascot of a heinie officers' brothel?"

"There's no such thing," the sergeant said. "The kid's a gold surveyor. I'll count to three."

"Count to hell," Booker said. "See if I care."

Romulus was laughing again. I didn't like that twitch between his eyes. "It's real quiet, and I got a heinie burp gun. I'll smoke you all and the pup, blame it on them rotten commandos that are looking for the Old Man. . . . One."

"I'm getting sore, Rom," Booker said.

"Two."

"My temperature's rising."

"Three."

I felt a wind at my side. A pistol banged in my ear. Romulus had a hole in his head. He died with that jackal's laugh on his lips. The little general had pulled the Colt out of my holster and shot the sergeant.

"I'll be damned," Booker said. "I'll be damned. We'll have to win the war with shooting like that. The general can really pull."

The Colt was already back under my belt when I slapped the little general.

Booker stared at me. "You're vicious. That boy saved your life."

I slapped him again. There was no expression on his face.

"Bookie, he's part of the scam. He sits on a tree stump, waiting for us. He's with the commandos. He's their lookout."

"You're crazier than Rom. He's a Gypsy brat that the officers have been banging."

"He's much, much more than a brat."

"You gonna question him in Hungarian or what?"

I didn't want to hit him again. "Herr General, where are the killer commandos?"

"In the Schloss," he said, like Lord Byron spitting poetry. Booker was amazed, but I wasn't.

"The baron was teaching you English, wasn't he?"

"Yes, Captain Kidd."

"And this was your training camp. You wanted to kill General Patton."

"Only capture him . . . or Willie."

"Why Willie?" Booker asked.

"To break Herr General Patton's heart and silence the music of his tanks."

"How many commandos are upstairs in the Schloss?"

"A hundred, sir."

"Rollie," Booker said, "let's call Command. The kid's a magician. And I don't like his mumbo jumbo."

"We don't need Command," I said. "We'll handle this ourselves. Just bring in our squad."

"It ain't the Wild West, Captain Kidd. Nigger MPs can freeze their butts off in these heinie hills."

"Sergeant, get on your horn."

"Bucket of Blood to Bunker Hill," Booker shouted into his field radio. I could never understand his mumbo jumbo. "Follow the blue crow five heartbeats to the west."

Our squad arrived in seven minutes. Nine military policemen. They looked at Romulus, didn't say a word.

"We'll need a friend in Graves Registration," Booker said.

"You're gonna make a missing person out of Rom?"

"Something like that, Captain Kidd. You have a better solution? He was socked in the head with the general's own gun. And who's gonna believe that some little Hungarian general smoked him?"

"Willie will believe it. Willie saw the whole thing."

"I doubt that a dog can testify at our court-martial, Captain Kidd."

"I'm not so sure. There've been stranger things in the ETO."

"Like what?"

"A phony castle on a hill." I nudged the kid. "Come on."

"We gonna surround that old Schloss?" Booker asked.

"No. I'm taking that castle with the kid."

"Then why'd you ask me to bring in the other boys?"

"We have to look like an army, don't we? You think the commandos aren't watching us?"

"And you wanna scare them with the boogeyman, nigger MPs?"

"Exactly," I said. "A black army all our own."

"Captain Kidd, if I didn't know you better, I'd have to include you in the category of white trash."

"We don't have time to moralize, Bookie. I'm taking the Schloss."

I started shoving the general up the hill. He was holding the handle of his silver dagger. I'd already seen what this kid was capable of. He could have knifed me in the neck and run on home. But he didn't have a home, unless it was that goddamn Schloss. It hung over our heads in its own blue mist, and for a second I almost believed that Count Dracula

22

had moved to Germany and was sitting out the war in a rented castle. I didn't care. The general could have been Dracula's assistant. I was taking the Schloss.

"If you poke me with the dagger, kid, I'll still have enough strength in me to break your bones. Is that clear?"

"Yes, Captain Kidd."

"You're gonna knock on the door and persuade the commandos to come out with their hands in the air. We have two grenade launchers. You know what that means? I can reduce that Schloss into a burning tower."

"Yes, Captain Kidd."

A bony head bumped against my knee.

"Christ." Willie had climbed up the hill. I couldn't chase him back down to the jeep. We'd have lost our initiative. The commandos would laugh at a soldier coddling a white pup.

The kid hunkered near the castle door. I heard him whisper. The door opened. I didn't even grab my Colt. Willie growled. Women and children marched out of the Schloss with their hands clasped behind their heads. And then I saw the commandos themselves. Withered men with unruly beards. These weren't heinies. They were Hungarians dressed in green, officers and enlisted men. The heinies had stripped them of their belt buckles and their boots. They didn't have a pistol among them, only a few silver daggers, just like the kid. They'd come to war with their wives and children, who stared at Willie and crossed themselves.

The wire services picked up our little tale. How could I have avoided marching those Hungarians into our camp? I had enough wits to collect the American uniforms and pile them into our jeep. Bookie and I and our squad of MPs had become big-time heroes with the pup. We'd captured the commandos *and* their children. The Old Man wasn't too happy about it. He couldn't even hang the Hungarians, because they weren't wearing American uniforms when we captured them. They weren't spies, only pathetic prisoners of war, and it cost the Third Army a fortune to feed them.

Bookie and I couldn't seem to part with the little general. We didn't give him up to G-2. Willie had already stopped growling in his presence. We lent him one of our uniforms, let him live in our jeep. No one took much notice of him. He blended into the usual chaos of army life.

I didn't mourn Romulus Rivers. He was lying somewhere in an unregistered grave. Who would have connected him to the heroes of the Hungarian campaign? I had Red. She was the one I cared about. And the Old Man. But the Green Hornet began to worry me. He was itching to grab Berlin.

"I want the big casino," he said.

"Georgie, just move in that direction, and Topside will pull you out of your seat and take away all your stars."

"I wish Pershing was at SHAEF."

"Black Jack" Pershing had been commander of American troops during the First War, with Georgie as one of his aides.

"Pipe dreams," I said. "Pershing is eighty-five years old."

"But he knew how to pick his staff. 'Georgie,' he said, 'I like generals so bold that they are dangerous.' And Ike keeps me in a cage. If I could get to Berlin, I'd grab Hitler and shoot that son of a bitch like I would a snake. . . . Rollie, why the hell did you bring my pup near a bunch of Hungarians?"

"I had to exercise him, sir."

"Then couldn't you have let him bite their biggest general?"

"They were starving, sir. And I didn't want to mingle his spit with theirs. It wouldn't have been fair to the pup."

I went outside Georgie's trailer. I was hungry for Margaret. But she was delivering doughnuts, like some angel of mercy with red hair.

"You shouldn't play cards with the Green Hornet."

"Why not?"

"Because it gives him ideas, and now he thinks Berlin is the big casino."

"But it *is* the big casino."

"Not for the Old Man. He can't have that bundle. Topside won't give it to him. Berlin is Stalin's show."

"Couldn't you write a letter to SHAEF?"

"Fat chance," I said. "Who would read it? I'm not Georgie's official aide-de-camp. I'm his scribe."

"A scribe who runs around with military policemen."

"Red, that's just an accident of war. . . . I love you. If I had to spend the rest of my life in Germany, I would, long as you'd remain a doughnut girl."

"You're ridiculous, Rollie. I didn't come into the ETO to fall in love with a half-wit. That's another accident of war."

"Do we have the truck tonight?"

"Don't be a pig. It's Sarah's turn. She has a new beau."

"Then we'll sleep in the war tent. I can arrange it."

"And what if the Old Man wakes up in the middle of the night and wants to study his maps?"

"Then we'll keep him company."

"Soldier," she said, "I have to go back to work."

She tugged my ears, kissed me on the mouth, and returned to her truck. I didn't even have a chance to recover from my dream of Red. Lieutenant Gabriel arrived with his boss, Powder Burns Monroe, Patton's G-2. Powder Burns hated me because I hadn't gone to West Point. I was a ninety-day wonder, like Lieutenant Gabriel, but he only hated me. He figured I was a little too tight with Willie and the Old Man. He was called Powder Burns because his pants and coat had caught on fire once in the middle of a war game in Tennessee.

"How's the hero?" he asked.

I wasn't afraid of Powder Burns. The Old Man wouldn't let him ride rough over me. He was a full colonel at thirty-five, belonged to that country club of career officers, but I didn't give a damn how meteoric his rise had been. I was the Green Hornet's confidant.

"That Hungarian incident wasn't my fault, sir."

"Yes it was, Captain Kidd. We're putting in your papers. You're going stateside starting tomorrow."

"Is that an order from the Old Man?"

"The Old Man has nothing to do with it. You almost got him killed."

"How? By capturing a load of Hungarians?"

"Rollie, you're the one who got captured. Those hunkies were only a trick. They kept you from locating the real thing. You stumbled onto Castle Höllenhund."

"A slave labor camp."

"With an underground city that's supposed to be Hitler's hotel after he gets bombed out of Berlin. . . . Meanwhile it was housing German commandos."

"I don't believe it."

"Lieutenant Gabriel," Powder Burns said, "should we enlighten the young man?"

We got into Powder Burns' jeep, and Gabriel drove us to the laager. But we didn't have Willie sitting up front with us. And we all had to sing out "Betty Grable" at least seventeen times.

There were corpses lying all over the place, heinies in their own helmets and GI winter coats, with wads of paper money falling out of their pockets.

"We had to smoke them in the tunnels," Powder Burns said, "one by one."

The laager was a labyrinth of trapdoors. We climbed down into tunnels I could never have imagined. I saw the largest barbershop in the world, with five hundred chairs. I saw rooms stacked to the ceiling with gold bars. I saw a bank that consisted of enormous barrels of currency. I saw bathtubs made of blue marble, and I wondered what the hell this war had been about. Were the Nazi princes going to vanish from the world with a couple of Loreleis and discover heaven in a refrigerated tomb?

I couldn't bear to be in this tunnel town. I had a coughing fit, and I ran out of that stinking laager. Powder Burns was smoking a cigarette.

"Rollie, you can sing to the Old Man. He might save your ass. You've been stealing cognac."

"Prove it," I said.

"Do you really want the inspector general to march into our war tent and hassle the Old Man? You shamed yourself. Do we have to dig around for a missing sergeant, huh? Let the dead stay dead. George should never have invited you onto his staff. You know how to charm, you ninety-day wonders. But we don't raise thieves at the Point."

I hit him, I struck Powder Burns. He smiled with blood and spit in his mouth.

"Rollie," Gabe said.

"Lieutenant Gabriel, it's all right. . . . Captain Kidd, we'll have to invent a death in the family. Your father? Mother? Favorite aunt? I'll expect you to be packed by oh six hundred hours. And no long good-byes. We'll explain the situation to George."

We drove back to camp. It was after midnight. I blundered into my MPs' tent. Booker rubbed his eyes. The little general was staying with them. I picked him out of his sleeping bag, held the Colt between his eyes. He didn't blink. His gaze was as fierce as mine.

"Admit it. You're a Nazi spy."

"Captain Kidd," Booker said, "you're disturbing our little brother."

"You took him in?" I growled at Booker Bell.

"Who else would? This tent is nigger country. And you're just one more white man from the world."

They were watching me, my own MPs, soldiers I'd assembled. Josh Hill, Zeke Hammer, Mordecai Jones . . .

I put the Colt away. The little general lunged at me with his silver dagger. Zeke plucked him out of the air, like you'd catch a football, and hurled him into the corner with his knife. "You be good, hear?"

"Don't you get it?" I said. "He's an assassin."

"Hitler be hiring Gypsies these days?" Zeke said.

"He belonged to the commandos. He was their whore, and–"

"Slave child, boss. There's a difference."

"I'm not your boss," I said.

"Then what you be calling a white captain in the United States Army?"

I'd never been inside their "country," never bothered to realize the aloneness of that tent. I couldn't accuse the little general, couldn't even say good-bye to Booker. I called him out of the tent.

"Bookie, get rid of every bottle of cognac we have."

"I already did. . . . They're sending you home, ain't they?"

We hugged in the dark, white man, black man.

"You'd better hide that little animal. Powder Burns is hot on the trail."

"Hot as horse manure. . . . It's got nothing to do with commandos, Rollie. He can't forgive that you're nearer the Green Hornet than he is, and you never went to West Point."

I searched for Red. But there wasn't a single doughnut girl inside their shelter. And I couldn't find the doughnut truck. The girls must have been on some midnight duty, delivering doughnuts and warm socks to tank boys a couple of forests away.

I had time to kill. I stood outside the Old Man's trailer, sucked on a cigarette with one of the guards. The lights were out. I wasn't going to wake up the Green Hornet. Then I heard a slight rumble inside the trailer. The door opened. Willie came out. His pink eyes roamed the turf. That pup had an uncanny instinct. He was a heartless dog, but whenever the notion hit him, he could be more human than any human being. He came up to me, bumped me with his nose. I could feel his anger and affection. He tolerated me on account of the Old Man.

"You take care of the Green Hornet, huh?"

I looked into his pink eyes. He knew I was leaving. He bumped me again with his nose and returned to the trailer.

RED

3

• She thought to kill herself, that's how she ached. She'd hop in front of the next whistle bomb, and those ghouls from Graves Registration would laugh. *That must be Red, the Green Hornet's little doughnut doll.* It was Margaret's one bit of immortality. She was like a maddened nun without Captain Kidd. She couldn't have known that his absence would leave such a large sucking wound. . . .

"Will you dance with me, Red?"

It was Mario English, *Time's* man in the ETO, who sweated like a pig under Patton's tent, around three colored riflemen with their own little combo. They weren't truckers or cooks, like the colored troops in the Seventh Army. They'd crossed the Rhine with hand grenades and broken clarinet reeds in their pockets, called themselves the Three Wicked Crows.

Margaret was dying to dance, but not with Mario English. She was hungry for her beanpole, her awkward Don Juan, who could never keep up with the Crows.

She could smell the bourbon on Mario's breath. He figured he had an open field.

"I'll fly you to Paris, Red. We'll stay at the Ritz, drink champagne."

"And have lunch with Ernest Hemingway?"

"Why not? I covered the Spanish war with Hem."

"The Ritz would have to prepare a magical meal, because Hemingway's in Havana."

"Hell," Mario said, "we'll visit him after the war. But dance with me."

There was such longing in his eyes that she had to twist her body away from Mario. She bumped into Powder Burns Monroe. He was delighted with himself. Georgie's G-2 had gotten rid of Roland.

"Red," he whispered, "I could get you a dozen pair of nylon underpants for one kiss in the doughnut truck."

"I'd rather kiss a snake."

Powder Burns was friendly with Colonel Gordon, Eisenhower's chief logistics officer, who could provide oranges for his own breakfast table, but not a gallon of gasoline for George. The whole Third Army was stalled, while the Canadians and the Brits were mounting their own amphibious operation, with a code name Margaret couldn't remember. It wasn't smart for Red Cross girls to discover too much about the Allied war machine. Suppose one of them was captured?

But she couldn't escape all her suitors. Private Willie shoved his bullet head between her ankles and slobbered all over Red. She'd rather dance with a dog than accept nylon underpants from Georgie's G-2. She stood Willie up on his hind legs and hopped around with him to the Wicked Crows. Willie was in paradise. He shut his pale eyes. And then he opened them in alarm. Private Willie had the best ears in the ETO. Lanterns started to blink. There was a slight jolt. And then she could hear that terrible halting whistle of a German rocket. Willie darted out of the tent.

The bomb exploded in the next field, far enough from Lucky Forward (the code name of Georgie's command). But the Three Wicked Crows unscrewed their clarinets. Margaret grabbed her helmet and ran to the nearest ditch. She was much less suicidal after dancing with a dog.

Hitler wanted to ruin Lucky's morale with his robot bombs. But he couldn't get to George. The general sat outside his trailer, with a cigar and a bottle of bourbon, Willie between his legs.

Mario, the man from *Time,* was curled next to Margaret in the ditch, crooning into her ear. She wasn't crazy about his hot bourbon breath. "Live with me, Red. You don't have a future with Captain Kidd. I'm here with you, and he's in the States, making money from the war."

She banged Mario in the ribs. "And what are you doing with your bylines, Mario? Feeding orphans?"

Margaret climbed out of the ditch and walked to the general's trailer.

"Buzz bombs," he said. "What the hell? If I get hit, I won't have to wear my uniform. No more buttoning and unbuttoning. . . . I miss Rollie. Can't write a letter without him. And I'm terrified of making a speech. His favorite aunt picked a rotten time to die."

"There was no aunt," she said. "It was Powder Burns, that blue-balled prick."

The general started to laugh. "Margaret, I admire your vocabulary. . . . It wasn't Powder Burns. It was Ike's staff. I was getting too frisky for SHAEF. Wouldn't listen to Ike's censors. Had my own speechwriter. Topside took him away."

"Couldn't we get him back?"

"And risk a war with the supreme commander? I'm already in the doghouse. God, I wish I had some gasoline. We're like an army of lost elephants. But you don't have to suffer. I could ship you home to Rollie."

"And share a room with his fiancée? Thank you, general. But I'll drink coffee with you in Berlin."

He scratched his white hair. His eyes were as pale as the pup's. He had the pinkest skin she'd ever seen on a man. They were like one person, the general and his dog.

"Don't say Berlin. They won't even let me cross into Czechoslovakia. I could take Prague in twenty-four hours. But Ike has me in his own special prison. We sit and wait for the Russkies. I feel like a bird in a room who can see outside through the window and beats himself to death trying to get out."

"General," she told him, "I'm that same bird."

There were no more cries from the clarinets. The dance had already disintegrated. She accompanied George to dinner. She ate in his tent with the other Red Cross girls. He'd invited Powder Burns and a few of the senior correspondents to sit with him. Mario English stroked Red's thigh under the table. She jabbed him with a fork, and the stroking stopped.

Powder Burns started to brag. "General, how many times have we caught the heinies with their pants down? We break

36

their codes, listen to all their traffic. We're practically sitting on Hitler's toilet seat."

"And how close are you to the toilets at SHAEF?"

"SHAEF, sir? I don't understand."

"Who the hell stole Captain Kidd from me?"

"His aunt died. . . . We had to act."

"Was it so crucial, Colonel, that he couldn't say good-bye to Red and me?"

"He was stealing, sir . . . from the German depots. Had his own black market. He was stabbing us in the heart."

"With liebfraumilch?"

"It got much worse than that. There's a missing supply sergeant." He leaned toward the general. "Sir, there are correspondents at the table."

"I invited them to dinner. We supply the candlelight. Are you calling Rollie a murderer?"

"No, sir. But he wasn't a true patriot. He was working for himself. There's this Nazi officer running around in an American uniform."

"The mythical major from the Waffen-SS."

"Müller is more than a myth. He rescued Mussolini. Stole him right off a mountain with a fleet of glider planes. Müller was hiding at Castle Höllenhund. Rollie went there to sack the place, tipped Müller off. We captured most of his men, but not the major."

"Is he going to whisk me off to Berlin in one of his glider planes? Then where the hell are my colored bodyguards?"

"I had to reassign them, sir. They were part of Rollie's gang. They're still MPs. But they're guarding the mess hall.

I had to make sure that Müller doesn't poison our soup."

The general gulped his bourbon and tossed a piece of toast at his G-2, who didn't dare to duck. The toast smacked him on the side of his head.

"What did Ike tell you? To isolate the Old Man, surround him with honchos from SHAEF? Jesus, I can't even have my own bodyguards. Get Rollie on the horn."

"He's stateside, sir. In New York."

"I don't care. That's your problem."

"The heinies will listen to every word. I can't . . ."

There was a great deal of noise outside the tent. Soldiers started to cheer. "Colonel, what's that ruckus all about?"

Powder Burns rushed from the table and returned with a fat grin. "General, it's a convoy filled with rations. We won't have to eat Spam morning and night."

The general tossed another piece of toast. "I'll hang the next man who brings me food. Give us gasoline."

He gulped more bourbon.

Red heard the shrill music of a robot bomb. She wanted to jump under the table, where Willie was. But she didn't move. She ate and drank with the general, while the bomb exploded and shook the tent. The lamps went out, and the candles leapt off the table. They sat in the dark until Powder Burns located the candles and relit them. The general had an awful shine on his pink face. The bourbon had gotten into his eyes. He'd drunk a whole quart. She was worried that he couldn't stand up, that he'd have to play the fool in his own tent.

"Margaret," he whispered, "will you walk Willie and me to our trailer?"

The other girls were jealous. They'd worn their best uniforms to dinner, with scarves and white gloves, had gobbled bits of canned duck to be near the general, to bask in the unsteady glow of the candles, and he hadn't invited them to walk him home. Sarah Tilsit stared at Red. She was from Oklahoma. She'd confided in Red, had dreams of sleeping with the general, of having him kiss her in the unholiest places. She'd have little bumping orgasms in the middle of her tale.

Margaret grabbed the general, lifted him off his chair, and half carried him to the mouth of the tent, while every soldier in sight saluted him, and she wondered if she'd have to be hospitalized with a hernia. But the general found the rhythm of his own two feet.

The Three Wicked Crows stood outside the tent with their clarinets, sucking very dark cigarettes. Their eyes were as bloody as the general's. They saluted him with their clarinets.

"Evening, general."

"Hello, boys," he said. "I enjoyed the music. But I can't jitterbug. I've fallen off too many horses to hop like that."

"It's all right, general. Private Willie danced with Red."

"Son of a bitch," the general muttered with a smile. "I've been outmaneuvered by my own dog."

He didn't need bourbon. He was their Georgie. And they'd die for him, or croon on a clarinet.

He invited Margaret into his trailer.

"General, I won't watch you drink."

"I finished my bottle," he said. "We'll play casino."

"Excuse me, but I wouldn't enjoy beating a blind man."

"Who's blind?"

Margaret took out her deck, held a four of diamonds in his face. "Describe that card if you can."

He started to squint and sway against the trailer door. "You're right. I can't see a thing. But will you keep me company for a while?"

There was a carbine on the general's cot.

"Are you taking target practice with the pup?"

"I'm not that drunk. It's a precaution. . . . I promised Ike. His G-2 insists that Major Müller is out there in the dark. He can crack through any position, kidnap my trailer."

"We'll stick doughnuts into his mouth until he suffocates."

"Negative. I'm not wasting good doughnuts on a phantom kraut."

"Then we'll use the same strategy on Powder Burns and finish him off."

"Now you're thinking like a soldier. Was your dad in the army, Red?"

"No, General. He's a fireman in Minneapolis. He fell off a ladder and sat out this war."

"And you went off to Wellesley with other firemen's daughters." The general wasn't drunk any more.

"No, sir. I was unique. The only fireman's daughter in my class."

The bookworm who had fancy notions about culture in an Eastern college. She was much too fine for Minneapolis. Red played Hamlet in high school. Not Ophelia, or the queen, but Hamlet himself, with her hair cropped short and tights that hugged her legs and nearly gave her drama coach a heart attack. He had palpitations looking at Princess Hamlet. She was all over Shakespeare. But it didn't really matter how many skulls she rattled on stage, how many gravediggers she argued with, how many kings she had to kill. She didn't have the right wardrobe for Wellesley. Firemen's daughters aren't good debutantes. Red didn't have money behind her, or an uncle in the diplomatic corps. She roomed with another wild girl, who had to count her pennies like Red did. They were outlawed from the important cliques. All the Shakespeare in the world couldn't help Red understand their idiotic language. They talked about homecoming balls, boys from Harvard they intended to marry. She memorized the little sermons of her profs, their own fanatical belief in the worth of Wellesley, but she was still Margaret Young, the freckle-faced drudge.

"I had a crisis, General. I nearly flunked out of Wellesley."

"But you got in on your own steam. My dad had to bribe two senators to get me into West Point."

"And now you're breaking Hitler's back."

"Without a gallon of gasoline. . . . But I'll say a prayer to your college. It was Wellesley that brought you to us."

"Yes, General, as a doughnut dolly. That's my destiny."

"Shush," he said. "My boys depend on you."

"And my flaming red hair."

She shivered where her heart should have been. She had no heart. It belonged to Captain Kidd. Red could feel the print of his body against hers. It was worse than drug addiction. Should she count the officers and correspondents who tried to get into her pants with promises of a weekend away from the war? But she was attached to her doughnut truck and a gentle pirate. Roland promised nothing but the liebfraumilch he loved to steal.

"Here." The general handed her a pocket pistol, a snubnosed Italian .32 he'd carried around with him since his days in Sicily.

"What's it for?"

"Protection."

"Against the man who rescued Mussolini?"

"Müller," the general said.

"But the Red Cross doesn't issue sidearms to its senior or junior canteen officers."

"That's why I'm giving it to you. I outrank the Red Cross."

"But I wouldn't know how to fire it."

"Shut your eyes and shoot. You'll hit something."

"Major Müller, I suppose."

"Keep it," he said. "Just in case. I'll feel better."

He touched his forehead, lay back on the cot, with Private Willie under his legs. Willie wasn't watching his master. His pale eyes were on Margaret.

The general started to groan. "How long, Lord, how long?"

"What's the matter, sir?"

"I'm praying to God for gasoline. . . . I am blind, Margaret. Would you help me undress?"

She got him out of his breeches and boots.

"I'm cold," he said.

Margaret lay down next to him on the cot and listened to him slumber in her arms. He slept like a baby.

4

• She was notorious after that. The other girls called her "Kay Summersby." Kay was Eisenhower's redheaded driver, a tall and beautiful Brit. . . . No, she wasn't a Brit. She was an Irish lady. There'd been rumors about a big, big romance. But Kay Summersby was none of Red's business. Red didn't drive General Patton around. She visited his trailer, sang him to sleep. He never touched her. It was Private Willie who delighted in digging his nose between her legs. The general would wake up and slap Willie's ears. "Young man, consider yourself confined to quarters. You're under arrest."

The general would go back to sleep, and Private Willie was so chagrined, he'd close those pale eyes of his with his own two paws.

The Third Army couldn't forage much with its trickle of gasoline. The general's tanks had to raid and run. But it was on one of these raids that his tankers had stumbled onto Buchenwald. The general wouldn't let Margaret near that death camp. He locked the door of his trailer and drowned himself in bourbon. He wouldn't accept calls from SHAEF. But he had his doughnut dollies drive to the compound where he'd put some of the camp's population. Margaret didn't see a single woman or child, just walking skulls in crazy German pajamas, men whose features had shrunk into their faces and left nothing but huge cannibal eyes. They couldn't eat solid food. She had to mash the doughnuts and serve them a kind of mush. She wasn't with them more than an hour. They clutched her hands, called her "angel" in Hungarian and other languages. She couldn't stop crying. Most of them were Margaret's age, but they looked like grandfathers who'd lived all their lives in a poisoned box.

One of the ancient young men picked Shakespeare's sonnets out of her pocket, kept pawing the book as if it were gold.

"Read to us, kind lady," he said.

But she couldn't read or recite one of Hamlet's songs. She lent him the book. The dollies returned to the doughnut truck, forgot about lunch or dinner, wouldn't have washed for a week if the general hadn't visited them.

"Girls, I need your help. Gordon is coming."

The god of gasoline. Margaret wanted to wiggle close to Gordon, charm his pants off, and set fire to Germany with Gordon's gasoline. That was how the doughnut dollies would have ended the war.

But George asked them to improvise a small canteen, so they could entertain Gordon's staff while he himself harangued Gordon and squeezed gasoline out of him.

"General, what will happen to those men in gray pajamas?"

"Girls," he said, "I just don't know."

"Will they live or die?"

His pale eyes began to twitch. "I just don't know . . . but they'll live a lot longer if we have some fuel."

They turned their tent into a canteen. The Three Wicked Crows arrived with their clarinets, and the dollies hopped with their own supply officers and Gordon's men. That's when Margaret saw Rollie's old MP, Booker Bell. He wasn't wearing his armband. He didn't even have a clarinet, like one of the Crows. He was serving hors d'oeuvres the dollies had prepared. She hugged him, because even without his armband, Booker reminded Margaret of her missing pirate.

"Sergeant Bell, why aren't you out chasing heinies in the forest?"

"I lost my status, Red. Powder Burns took away my stripes."

"I'll kill him for you."

"That won't bring Rollie back."

Both of them mourned that beanpole. The Third Army didn't make much sense without him. Red wouldn't monopolize Booker Bell. She had to let him continue his chores. But she couldn't get enthusiastic about Gordon and his supply officers when she had a hole in her heart called Captain Kidd.

A sergeant slipped into the tent. He wore the insignia of SHAEF. He danced with Sarah, hugged her a little too close, but Sarah didn't seem to mind. She preferred him to all the officers in the tent. He had light brown hair, and Red could almost feel the muscles under his tunic.

He dropped Sarah, grabbed Red's hand, and pulled her away from one of the officers.

"Freckles, you're mine."

He shouldn't have been dancing in a tent full of officers.

"Are you Gordon's driver?"

"Backup driver," he said. "Name is Farnsworth, Bruce."

"Well, Farnsworth, Bruce, this is an officers' hop."

"And I'm a noncommissioned officer. Ol' Gordon can't live without me."

"But I can," she said.

Gordon's driver laughed. "How's Joe Louis?" he asked. "The Brown Bomber. I thought he was the Old Man's secret weapon."

"I've never seen Joe Louis in Patton's tent."

There was something strange about Farnsworth, Bruce. He didn't hug her greedily like Gordon's other officers. He was savage and tender at the same time, and he danced like a continental. Margaret had her pocket pistol and was prepared to shoot his eyes out if he was masquerading as an NCO.

"Soldier," she said, "where are you from?"

"Manhattan, Kansas."

She knew her terrain like one of Georgie's tankers. "Did you ever go boating on the Big Blue?"

"Lots of times, Freckles. But what makes you so interested in a dinky river?"

"That's the problem, Sergeant Farnsworth. The Blue is very shallow the closer you get to Manhattan."

"It can still support a canoe."

And he tossed her between his legs, like a rubber doll. She was much too dizzy to ask him more questions. And before she could get her balance back and look him in the eye, Farnsworth had disappeared. She was worried about her general, but there were guards stationed outside his war tent, and a phony sergeant couldn't have gotten in no matter what insignia he wore.

In an hour Gordon and his men were gone, and her general didn't seem pleased. Gordon had promised him the sky, but they still had no gasoline. And her general had to send out scavengers to steal gasoline from the Seventh Army.

"We could sure use Captain Kidd," he said.

And she didn't want to bother him with her suspicions. Would Major Müller have come wandering into one of their canteens like that? He now had a code name: Mandrake the Magician, because of his power to camouflage himself, to hide in the dust and smoke. But at least Mario English stopped pawing her. He had to be careful. She was the general's lady. That's what he thought.

"How are you, Kay Summersby?"

"Fit as a peach," she said.

"Patton's peach."

She socked him on the jaw. His eyes wandered in his head. He was in shock. He hadn't expected the general's lady to be so unladylike.

"Whore of Babylon," he said, when he fully woke up. "I'll write about you in my column."

"That's wonderful. I'll have a fan club."

But she was a pariah. None of the officers would dare flirt with Red. And the doughnut dollies formed their own clique. It was like being back at Wellesley. Sarah was the coldest of them all. Red had robbed her of her general. And she couldn't convince Sarah that her liaison with Georgie Patton was through a deck of cards. She played casino half the night, while Willie licked her ankles when his master wasn't looking.

During the day, Sarah and Margaret shuttled between headquarters and that compound where the skeletons lived. Margaret stopped mashing doughnuts. She fed them coffee and milk, oranges and candy bars. And she would recite *Hamlet* to whatever refugees wanted to listen. They were the best audience Margaret had ever had.

Shakespeare had never come into the camp. Poetry was an exotic gift, like oranges from Africa or peanut bars from Hershey, Pennsylvania. She grew attached to the ancient young men, even if it was hard to look at their blue skulls.

She would drive the truck, with Sarah next to her, always silent. Sarah wouldn't reveal her dreams now that Red was Kay Summersby.

"Sarah, I'm not sleeping–"

"Shut up."

And it was on one of the refugee runs that she spotted Sergeant Farnsworth, caught him pissing behind a tree.

He jumped onto the road and started to wave her down. She hit the accelerator. Sarah screamed. "Are you crazy, Red? You'll ruin that soldier."

But Farnsworth was much too nimble for them. He leapt onto the running board on Sarah's side of the truck, opened the door, clutched Sarah's scalp, and tossed her into their little galley.

Margaret hissed at him. "Major Müller."

He tried to grab the wheel.

Sarah started to cry. "I don't understand. I don't understand."

"Major, how's life with the Waffen-SS?"

"I'm from Hamburg, Freckles, not Berlin." And he walloped her on the side of the head. Red's ears were ringing, but she still clutched the wheel. "I'm with German intelligence."

"Hitler's G-2."

"We despise Uncle Adolf." And he walloped her again. "Freckles, give me the wheel."

"What were you doing in our canteen?"

"I saw you," he said. "I couldn't resist."

"But you danced with Sarah first," she said.

"I had to find a decoy."

Sarah continued to cry. "I don't understand. Isn't the sergeant a soldier boy? He danced with me to get to you."

"That's German intelligence," Margaret said with blood on her lip.

Müller seized the wheel. "You'll both behave. I'm Sergeant Farnsworth, on loan to the Red Cross." He reached back with his free hand and clutched Sarah's scalp again. "Freckles, I'll tear her head off. I mean it. You'll salute when we get to the checkpoints. And we'll drive up to the general's trailer."

"Of course," she said. "Like clockwork." She pulled out the pistol and aimed it at Müller, blew his ear away. There was blood all over the windshield. Müller howled and clutched his head. They swerved, and the major fell out of the truck.

She drove like the devil to George's command. He was almost clairvoyant. "Müller," he said, looking at the blood on her face. "Müller."

A hundred men searched for that major with the missing ear. They might have found him if only they'd had a little more gasoline.

She put Sarah to bed, rinsed herself under the little faucet that the dollies had behind their tent, scrubbed Müller off her skin. She started to cry. She had a general, a lecherous dog, and a poetry circle that consisted of blue skulls, but she'd never survive without Captain Kidd.

ROLAND

5

• Wrote to Red religiously twice a week. I knew the censors would pick at my prose; I didn't talk love. I told her how I wanted to be with Willie and the Green Hornet again. Red didn't write back, and once or twice a month my own letters would arrive in an envelope with the Third Army's stamp: ADDRESSEE UNKNOWN. It was horse manure, as Bookie would say. How could a doughnut girl get lost in a heinie forest? The ETO wasn't a German fairy tale, with Hansel and Gretel. Or was it?

I wrote to the Green Hornet just as religiously, but none of those letters ever came back. I even wrote to the pup, c/o General George Patton. And curiously, I got a reply. Some joker in G-2 sent me a form letter saying that Willie received so much fan mail he couldn't answer all his correspondents with a personal note. The joker had even copied Willie's paw print. But he didn't acknowledge that I'd ever served with the Green Hornet. I was the army's invisible man.

I could have lived with that if there hadn't been such a hullabaloo back home. I was the young officer who'd captured a hundred commandos with a handful of colored MPs and General Patton's dog. I had to speak at women's clubs, wear my uniform. Then Hitler died in his bunker, the Russkies took Berlin, and my father treated me to a magnificent lunch with his entire firm. My fiancée was there, of course. Lizabeth Rose, who had enough manners not to rush a soldier into marriage. She was the biggest catch among the Karps and the Kahns. Lana Turner without the bleached blond hair, and a dowry that was almost obscene. I might have loved her all my life if I hadn't met Red in the ETO.

I wrote to Wellesley College, but the registrar didn't have her address. I searched the Minneapolis phone book, found two hundred and seven listings under Red's family name. *Young.* I scribbled to every one, hoping I'd stumble upon some lost uncle or aunt. But none of these Youngs ever wrote back.

Georgie, the fighting general, was named military governor of Bavaria, and I felt in my gut that it was a form of suicide. He was no politician, and he was helpless without his lightning runs. The general who had liberated Buchenwald seemed a little too close to the Nazis now. He would mumble about "Semites and Mongol hordes." One of my father's senior partners invited me into his office. He'd lost a son at Omaha Beach.

"Rollie, I'm no more religious than you are . . . but if he's been making remarks . . . You served with the son of a bitch."

"He saved lives, Mr. Lieberman. He had to rescue Eisenhower at the Battle of the Bulge. If you'd seen him as a soldier, sir, you'd forgive whatever craziness was in his head."

But the army couldn't forgive George. He lost his command. He was given toy soldiers to play with, the Fifteenth Army, which had no tanks or troops, and he started writing a memoir of the war in Europe. He didn't even last out the year. He was planning to sail home in the middle of December, on the battleship *New York*. But first he went on a hunting trip. His car collided with a two-and-a-half-ton truck. George cracked his head against the partition that separated him from his driver. He severed his spine and was nearly scalped. "I think I'm paralyzed," he said. He was taken to a hospital in Heidelberg, where he died just before Christmas. There was a photo in the papers of Willie sitting like a warrior next to the Old Man's trunk.

I married Lizabeth in February of '46. It wasn't her fault that she didn't have freckles. The moments I made love to her I did manage to forget about Red. We honeymooned in the Bahamas. My life seemed all set. Lizabeth's parents bought us an apartment on Fifth Avenue, a couple of buildings away from where I'd grown up with Mom and Dad. I forgot about Harvard Law. I couldn't have grubbed around with books after I'd lived inside a war tent. Dad wanted me to join his firm, not as some trainee, but as a former army captain who would inherit Kahn & Kahn. I didn't want to handle other people's money. I was a pirate, after all, a dealer in cognac who never made a dime for himself. And so I took over Mom's department store, Karp & Co., which was right on Union Square. It had once been the rival of Macy's and Gimbel's, but now it was just another dinosaur. Manhattan didn't shop at Karp & Co. The smartest people visited the green-and-amber balconies at Macy's, climbed through the looking glass into an Art Deco world. Our clients came from Washington Heights and the Bronx, hunting for bargains in the deep caverns of Karp & Co. Mom was a little ashamed.

"We'll sell the old girl. Rollie, it's not for you. It will collapse under your heels one day."

But Lizabeth socked her own money into the sinking ship. She was already pregnant with our child, and she wanted her husband to be happy with Karp & Co. She imagined a downtown Macy's, with amber balconies of its own. Architects were called in. We planned to close shop for six months, build a new facade, rip out the floors, and put in escalators that reached to the sky. And in the midst of the furor, I found a bundle on my desk at Karp & Co. I opened the bundle. It was packed with letters from George. The Green Hornet hadn't forgotten me. I started to cry as I examined the familiar crook of his hand. He wasn't much of a speller. He'd always relied on Rollie. He was a bit dyslexic, and so I would read to him and scribble the first draft of each letter he had to write.

He'd gone to the big casino after the war to meet with President Truman. "Rollie, Berlin gives me the blues." The pup sat under his chair even when he had to chat with other generals. "Willie's always looking around the corner, expecting to find a certain captain with his doughnut girl. That dog is fonder of you than you think. . . . There's a shortage of doughnut girls in Bavaria. I'd give a million to have a couple more like Red." I wasn't the only lost child. George and the pup had been as hungry for Red as I was. And he didn't even have his armored divisions. "Rollie, last time a war stopped

I wrote a poem. . . . Now I feel too low. Yours truly, The Green Hornet."

I didn't find one spelling mistake, but I couldn't stop crying. Our child was born, a wrinkled boy with a raw belly button. We called him Jonathan, after one of Lizabeth's forefathers. I couldn't bear to look at the boy. God help me, I didn't love him. I should never have married. I was a war orphan, an amnesiac, an ex-pirate. But my wife was patient with me. I'd hold baby Jonathan, grip his hand. I got used to him. But I had criminal thoughts. I wanted a baby with Red and no one else in the world.

I sent all the architects away. I wasn't going to rebuild Karp & Co. It was 1947, and Macy's had been immortalized in *Miracle on 34th Street*, a film about Santa's visit to the world's biggest department store. How could I compete? We kept the rotting staircases, and I expanded our bargain basement. If families came down from Washington Heights to shop at Karp's, we had to give them a reason.

We economized. I didn't even take a salary as president of Karp & Co. Lizabeth gave me whatever cash I needed out of her own pocket. I liked it that way. If I was a thief, I'd have to learn how to steal again.

I had a curious Christmas. Jonathan was six months old. I'd carry him perched on my shoulder like an owl. I brought him to the annual party at Karp & Co. He was still on my shoulder when I handed out bonuses to all my hundred and ninety-nine employees. Rosalind, my spinster secretary from Queens, had been guzzling champagne for half an hour. "Mr.

Kahn, there's a colored man in the corridor, asking for you."

"Invite him in, Roz. Invite him in."

Roz was petrified. Neither Macy's nor Gimbel's nor Karp's had a black clientele. Colored people didn't usually come downtown in 1947. Cops kept them out of Central Park below Ninety-sixth Street, which was like a dividing line between white and black heaven. I had colored janitors, but not a single colored clerk.

Roz followed my instructions and let the colored man into our office party. He wore smarter clothes than I had to sell. His shoes and tie were much too expensive for Karp & Co. His shirt was handstitched. I almost couldn't recognize him under that finery and his combed mustache. He was like a prince among red-faced barbarians. I hadn't seen Booker Bell in two and a half years.

"That your boy?" he asked, looking at Jonathan on my shoulder.

"Bookie, why did you wait so long?"

We hugged in front of my employees. Then I brought him into Roz's office and closed the door.

"You were our lucky charm, Captain Kidd. Powder Burns flopped us the day after you left. We couldn't even get near the Green Hornet. We had to police the kitchens."

"Ah, all I did was bring you bad luck."

"No, little man. I found a son because of you."

"Son? We stole cognac, shot at heinies, walked the pup."

"His name is Romulus Rivers Bell."

"Bookie, do you have to mention ghosts? I've had too much to drink."

58

"That little general ain't a ghost."

"The kid with the dagger? The Gypsy?"

"I adopted him," Booker said.

"You brought him back to America?"

"Right on our troopship. We fixed him up with dog tags. It was fine."

"My head is swimming. I can't keep up with you."

"It's simple, Rollie. He's a nigger, like us. We weren't gonna leave him in no German woods. I got me adoption papers, and we had to call him something. Why not Rom?"

"I'll tell you why not. Because your son shot Romulus Rivers."

"And saved your life," Booker said.

"Then I ought to kiss his toes, huh?"

"Rollie, I need a favor. I ain't fooling." There was terror in his princely eyes. I wouldn't have begrudged Booker Bell.

"Anything," I said, "long as it's only a little illegal."

"Rom's in the crud. I sent him to a private school in Harlem. You didn't know that we had our own schools and academies, did you?"

"Bookie, I've never been to Harlem more than once or twice."

"What's the matter with you, little man? No rent parties? No hot yellow mamas? No diddling at the Savoy?"

"Nothing that romantic," I said. "My dad and I had tea with some colored banker on Sugar Hill."

"The kid's been stealing from the academy. I have my pull. I paid off the school's president. But he ripped a boy with his knife."

"That same lousy dagger?"

"Didn't have the heart to take it away from him. It was like a piece of history. . . . The cops grabbed him and the knife. He's sitting in a cell. I would have fixed it with the judge, but he ain't black. My mojo doesn't mean much out in the World."

"And you want me to talk to the judge, smooth it over with him, considering that I'm a white man."

"And a war hero."

"Come on, Booker. That kid laid those Hungarians on us. The commandos were under the ground."

"A war hero," Booker insisted.

"Do I have to wear my uniform when I meet the judge?"

"No, Captain Kidd. Just come with me to his chambers. Lie for Brother Bell. Promise that white man that you'll take custody of Rom, that you'll raise him to be a banker or a clothing king."

"And what if that judge sends his people to my address?"

"Then I'll produce Rom. I got enough mojo for that."

I didn't have much sympathy for Booker's scheme until I discovered children's court. It was attached to a tiny jail on Elk Street, behind City Hall. I entered that jail, caught the little general in his cell. I wanted to have a look at him before I greeted the judge. He wasn't wearing lipstick on Elk Street or a winter coat. He should have stayed at Castle Höllen-hund. He hadn't grown an inch in America. He had the same futility on his face. I hadn't noticed that his eyes were as blue as the Green Hornet's. And I could understand why Booker had adopted such a little assassin. I might have adopted him myself under different circumstances. He was one of us, a war orphan. We didn't even say hello. That's how much we hated each other. But I couldn't let him live behind those crisscrossed bars, like an animal plucked out of the wild, frozen in time and place. The commandos had formed him. He'd never survive a colored academy in Harlem. But I couldn't tell Booker that. The kid's education had started and stopped in an officer's brothel.

I sang to the judge with Booker sitting silent on the other side of the chambers. The judge had a fireplace. He was a hack who'd been around since the First War. He had watery eyes and a winter cough. He was sucking lemon drops. His sustenance depended on bribes and political contributions. He didn't condescend to look at Bookie. But he couldn't keep his eyes off me. He knew all about my exploits in the ETO, about Dad's banking firm, about Karp & Co. He could smell money in his pocket.

He sat with the little general's dossier while I continued to sing. "Sergeant Bell served with me, Your Honor. He was a military policeman who guarded General Patton."

"But there's something suspicious here. A military policeman with a criminal record."

Booker had spent a month in the Tombs after a barroom brawl.

"How did he ever adopt this child?" the judge seemed to ask himself. His name was Van Horn, Vincent Van Horn.

"And the child is vicious. Where does he come from? I don't have a prior address. He knifes another boy, and I'm supposed to let him out of the court's sight?"

"Put him in my custody, Your Honor."

Vincent Van Horn sucked another lemon drop. The sound was unbearable.

"Mr. Kahn, are you sure you want to get involved?" He leaned toward me. "I swear to you. It's not regular. It's not right. A boy without a background. An adoptive father who's been in the Tombs."

"I'll take full responsibility."

"Kahn, the child isn't colored, is he?" Van Horn whispered in my ear.

"No, Your Honor."

"Then how did a colored man get claim to him, a colored man without a recognizable occupation or a wife?"

"Mr. Bell is a businessman, Your Honor."

"Eh? What sort of business?"

I had to spin faster than the judge. "He buys and sells for me."

"Why didn't you say so? A colored salesman for a Manhattan department store. That has to be a first."

"May I have the child, Your Honor?"

"It's your funeral, Kahn. I'll expect to see him once a month. We aren't slackers at children's court. We don't fall asleep in our chairs."

I wanted to hit him. And it was a wonderful feeling to be able to resist. We got Romulus Rivers Bell out of that children's jail, and Booker had never uttered a word. I brought them back with me to Fifth Avenue. I was the kid's custodian. I couldn't toss him and Bookie into the wind. Lizabeth Rose took a liking to my war buddy. She'd never met one of my MPs. She served Romulus a big slab of key lime pie. The kid didn't look at the furniture or the fireplace. He watched baby Jonathan, and I was scared to death. That assassin was jealous of my family life. He could have seized Jonathan, thrown him out the window. He masked his envy with an angelic smile.

"Let me hold him, Captain Kidd."

Lizabeth put our baby in the assassin's arms. I was on my toes, poised to attack. I couldn't stop gritting my teeth. Romulus rocked the baby, returned him to Lizabeth. I could fathom his commando language. He'd found my jugular, knew where and how to draw blood. I wanted to kill him. He left with Booker Bell.

"Darling," Lizabeth said, "why did that boy call you 'Captain Kidd'?"

"It was my code name, dear. Among the MPs. All officers were pirates to them. I was their particular pirate."

"But I watched his lips. He could have been calling you that all his life. Captain Kidd."

I started to tremble, couldn't stop.

"Rollie, what's wrong?"

"Nothing, dear," I said, propping Jonathan on my shoulder. "It's like malaria when I remember the war."

I put the baby to sleep, made love to Lizabeth, and my "malaria" went away. I should never have gone to that children's court. I should have run as far from Romulus Rivers Bell as I could. But the little assassin was in my blood. My thief's life was about to begin again.

There was an enormous shipment of men's and women's clothes waiting for Captain Kidd at Karp & Co., merchandise meant for Macy's. My clerks were dumbfounded, but it was pretty clear. Booker had hijacked Macy's trucks as a present for me. I found him in my office, watching the smoke rings he created with his Cuban cigar.

"Bookie, you want to start a truckers' war? I can't fight Macy's."

"I had to show my gratitude, little man. Without you, the courts would have swallowed up my son."

"But that's fifty thousand dollars' worth of clothes in my storeroom."

"Sixty," Booker said, "if you count my commission."

"Booker Bell, are you propositioning me?"

"I bleed Macy's, I bleed Gimbel's, but they'll never feel the loss of blood. My hemorrhages are very, very slow."

"But how the hell can I display Gimbel's goods?"

"Who has the biggest bargain basement in New York?"

"Karp's of Union Square."

"And a lot of goods can get lost in a basement."

"You expect my clerks to be your accomplices?"

"Relax, little man. I already ripped out the labels. Do you want the biggest bargain basement or the best?"

We were pirates, Bookie and I, in peace and in war. Suddenly I began to look forward to the new year. I'd found my lost brother, Booker Bell.

6

● We prospered in '48. I doubled my employees, while the country fell into a long recession. Our staircases continued to crumble. I could have ripped them out like a heartless surgeon, but I expanded our basement instead. We were drawing people from Macy's and Gimbel's. Suddenly I was a retailer to be reckoned with. I sat on five charitable boards. "What temple are you affiliated with?" the boards kept asking me.

"None."

"We don't care if you're Hindu or Episcopalian. But you have to have some rabbi or minister behind you. It's critical, Mr. Kahn."

I offered to resign. But I'd become too valuable, thanks to my silent partner, Booker Bell. Our turnover was terrific. Whatever moved into the basement moved out. Karp's began to appear in all the guidebooks. We were getting customers from Ohio and Buenos Aires. I was twenty-seven years old, and I thought of killing myself.

Went to my doctor. He was an old army man, but he hadn't served with us in the ETO. He examined my vital signs, said I was suffering from a delayed form of battle fatigue. Told him not to use those words. I didn't want to get slapped by Georgie's ghost. But I hee-hawed in my own miserable heart. How could a general's scribe catch such a disease? I'd been near the front lines, yes, and I often patrolled ahead of George on my cognac runs with Booker and the pup. But I didn't bump heads with the enemy, not very often. My spirit was leaking, a little at a time. I missed Red and the Old Man, couldn't seem to function at Karp & Co.

The doc wanted to put me in a VA hospital, have me observed by a bunch of specialists, but Mom wouldn't hear of it. "Roland shouldn't be around mental cases," she said. "He's a war hero."

She shipped me to a private clinic out on Long Island. "I'll run the store," she said. "Roland, you don't have to worry. We'll be fine."

I'd already kissed Lizabeth and baby Jon good-bye. I packed my toothbrush and pajamas. I met with psychiatrists, discussed my dreams, but my spirit continued to leak. The psychiatrists took away my belt and my razor. I wore a long white gown. The ocean was right outside my window.

Booker visited me. He was the only one who could read my gloom.

"Little man, you got the military blues. It's the worst case I've ever seen. But I brought you something." He shouted at someone behind his back. "William the Conqueror, come here!"

A dog strolled into the room. Booker was up to one of his tricks. It was a bull terrier, all right, but Willie had "retired" to a farm in Massachusetts with Georgie's widow. I'd read about it in the papers. I knew my facts. Booker had found a reasonable facsimile of the dog, and was trying to fob him off on Captain Kidd.

The mutt came near my bed. He didn't even have Willie's ferocious look.

"Booker, keep this mutt away from me. I don't want Willie's look-alike."

"Look-alike? You ought to be a little more gracious to the Green Hornet's dog."

"That ain't Willie," I said.

The dog bumped me with his nose. I looked into his eyes. How could I tell if he was Willie the warrior?

"Where'd you get him?"

"Damn you," Booker said. "I have my own pipeline."

"You stole the pup from Mrs. Patton?"

"Borrowed him," Booker mumbled. I didn't want him to suffer. I pretended that *his* Willie was the real thing. And it's peculiar, but having the pup around, whoever he was, cured me of my blues. I left the clinic with Willie, returned to Karp & Co.

The pup had grown attached to me. What if he got jealous of baby Jon? But he didn't growl at Jon, just ignored him and Lizabeth. He'd only answer to my call. I took him to work with me, shoved him under my desk. He wasn't ferocious, like the other Willie had been. He was no attack dog. His tail started to wag when he saw Booker again.

"Quite a little family," Booker said. "What's the matter? Still got the military blues?"

I wouldn't answer him. He sat on my desk. "Tell Brother Booker."

"I can't stop thinking of Red."

"Shame on you. A pillar in the world, with a gorgeous wife and child, and the general's dog, and you dream of doughnut girls."

"Find her for me."

Bookie had become my bill collector. His gang could locate anyone who had a delinquent account at Karp & Co. We didn't have to write off a single debt.

"You have the facilities. Couldn't your gang find Red?"

"Sure. If she had an unpaid bill, we'd track her down. But your Red doesn't exist. . . . Why don't you pay attention to some of the new girls?"

I let Bookie bring a couple of high yellow clerks into the basement. They could have come dancing out of the Cotton Club, though I'd never been near that mythic place and could only imagine what the dancers might have looked like. My other clerks grumbled, but they didn't rebel as long as I kept the high yellow clerks in the basement. Customers were crazy about them, and so was I, but their striking figures and startling clothes couldn't dislodge my memories of Red.

Romulus visited me. The kid seemed shorter than ever. He was wearing the dark blue blazer of his academy. "You got to speak to Dad. . . . I can't go to school."

"Rom, it's the American way. Booker only wants the best."

"I've killed people, Captain Kidd. I've set Russian PWs on fire. I've slept with a hundred German officers. How can

I sit on a hill with teachers who've been nowhere, with boys who've never seen their mama's bush?"

I couldn't tamper with his argument. The kid had a powerful point. "What can I do?"

"Tell Dad I want to join his gang."

"That's out of the question. You can't quit school until you're sixteen. The law won't allow it. And how can we get around Judge Van Horn? You're on probation, remember?"

"I'll steal," the kid said. "I'll go on a rampage."

I dreaded it. I knew I'd have to face Booker's wrath.

We went to Lüchow's, on Fourteenth Street. It was a heinie restaurant that thrived when lower Manhattan had been flooded with music halls, when mayors and governors and divas like Lillian Russell would eat there every night. I had my own table, of course, and no one challenged the presence of a black businessman like Booker Bell. We had the sauerbraten with applesauce and roasted potatoes that were out of this world, but the liebfraumilch couldn't compare with the Third Army's stolen stock.

"Bookie, don't get mad. Your kid wants to leave the academy . . . and join the Booker Bell gang."

My partner's cheeks began to shake. He would have murdered me in Lüchow's if he could. He pretended to smile.

"I'll be glad to, little man, when you invite baby Jon into the same gang."

He left the table, abandoned me. I didn't see him for a month. But he knocked on my door after one of the academy's buildings burned down.

He was crying. "Cruel man, you want to turn my own son into a criminal."

"That's the only career he's ever had. Maybe he'll grow out of it."

"Not one more word, Captain Kidd."

He tossed a folder on my desk.

"What is it?"

"Magic. Powder Burns' employment record and credit rating."

"I must be dumb. Since when does Georgie's old G-2 need credit ratings?"

"That's it. He ain't G-2. He's out on his ass. And the little mother has been borrowing all over the place to keep alive. That's how I got his folder. From my associates uptown. His credit stinks in Harlem too. I could have his legs broken, Rollie, or worse."

"He's looking for a job?"

"Yeah, as a department-store detective."

We didn't have detectives at Karp & Co. You couldn't really police a bargain basement. We just added five percent onto our annual budget for "slippage."

"Rollie, let's interview the mother. We'll have our revenge."

I didn't want to do it all alone. I had another desk put into my office for our little charade. Booker's desk was even bigger than mine. I had Roz call Powder Burns, arrange an interview.

Our joy went away. Without his uniform, he was just a balding man, close to forty, with gray lips. Him, the youngest colonel in history, with a future that should have been grander than mine. I looked at my silent partner. We didn't want revenge, only a couple of tiny twists before we tossed Powder Burns out of Karp & Co.

He saluted us, like we were the generals.

"Stop that," I said. "What the hell did they teach you at the Point?"

"Brother," Bookie said, "what do people call you when they aren't calling you 'Powder Burns'?"

"Robert, sir," he said, clicking his heels.

"Rollie, he's 'sirring' us now. . . . Robert, how did you get into the desperate condition where you are sucking up to a couple of men you were trying to destroy?"

"I never tried to destroy you, Booker."

"You didn't send Brother Roland stateside, while his sweetheart was giving out doughnuts to the Green Hornet's troops?"

"Doughnuts? I can't remember."

"Red. Her name was Red."

"But there was a missing supply sergeant."

"A recreant who was stealing gold. Does Brother Roland look like a poor man to you?"

"No. That's what disturbed me the most. Rollie is rich."

"Then wasn't it more like recreation, Brother Robert, filling the Third Army's coffers with free cognac? But how did you fall?"

"The Old Man got wind of what I had done. He couldn't seem to function without his scribe. He stopped writing letters."

I had to break in. "But what happened to *my* letters, the letters I wrote to Margaret Young?"

"They were left at our depot in Nancy. I asked the censors to sit on them."

"And did the censors sit on my letters to the Green Hornet?"

"They got to the Hornet eventually. We just didn't deliver the Hornet's reply."

"But his letters did come . . . after he died."

"That wasn't my doing. I was long gone from the ETO."

"Did Willie give you the evil eye?"

"No. Not Willie. When the generals saw I was in disfavor, they pounced. I killed a heinie during some interrogation. It was an accident. I hit him too hard with my pistol butt. It should have been hushed up. My own lieutenants squealed on me. I sat with the inspector general. I was given the choice: a court-martial or my commission."

"And you started to drink and drift, huh? How did you land in Manhattan?"

"It's the end of the world, far from Nebraska. Rollie, can you use a good security man?"

"Hold your horses," Bookie said. "You can't worm your way into Karp & Co. We have to give you an intelligence test. It consists of one question. If you were in harness again, if you could repeat your miserable past, would you kick out Captain Kidd?"

The pup came out from under my desk like a floating hallucination, growled at Georgie's G-2, and disappeared between my legs.

Powder Burns didn't blink. He stared at Booker and me. His mouth twitched, but he never lost his concentration.

"Would you, brother, would you do the same thing?"

"Yes."

We hired the son of a bitch. It was a selfish act. I wasn't going to give up a shrewd security chief. But I told him he couldn't arrest anyone. We weren't dealing with heinies. He could keep a small room in the basement, where he was allowed to "invite" a customer to enter. But the room couldn't have any bars or a lock. And he must never accuse a man or a woman of theft. Karp's had "spillage," not thievery. He could pursue, but never pounce. Nor could he call in the police. Karp & Co. would talk to its shoplifters, take them to tea.

Powder Burns fell right into the policy of the store. Our "spillage" went down to three percent. He roamed our basement with the eagle eye of a West Point graduate. When Karp & Co. "integrated" the store, encouraged shoppers to come down from Harlem in our very own bus, which Bookie supplied, Powder Burns defended me with his own implacable logic.

"If the Brooklyn Dodgers have Jackie Robinson, Karp's can have a Harlem bus."

"But remember what happened when Filene's tried to integrate," said my bookkeeper about Boston's own spectacular bargain basement. "There was civil war."

"Boston is backward country," Powder Burns answered.

"The home of the American Revolution," said my Jewish bookkeeper.

"We're beating Gimbel's to the punch."

"Gimbel's doesn't have to depend on its basement. We do."

But when we had Jackie Robinson visit Karp's, there was barely room to breathe. Our white shoppers didn't stray. Booker pumped in more stolen merchandise. We had a second Harlem bus. We hired more colored clerks, not those fabulous Cotton Clubbers, but girls fresh out of Harlem high schools, who didn't look like they'd come from a chorus line.

We had hate mail and one bomb scare, but that's as far as the fury went. We ended the year with galloping receipts. I didn't monkey with the chandeliers. I gave out bigger bonuses. I learned to love baby Jon. I'd have ripped out the throat of anyone who harmed him, meaning Romulus Rivers Bell. I admired my rich, sexy wife, a bombshell who would have driven other men wild. We were named Couple of the Year by the Downtown Merchants' Association. We danced together at the merchants' ball, her skin gleaming in the dark, like some voluptuous tigress. I was twenty-eight years old, a war veteran, a man on the rise, with a bargain basement that was beginning to scare Macy's and Gimbel's. Merchants kissed my hand. None of it was real to me. I'd only been alive near the Green Hornet and Red. Karp's was a cavern to me, like the tunnel town of Höllenhund. I always had a little vertigo when I entered that cave without a window. But I wasn't reckless. I played the husband, the father, the clothing king.

. . .

We had to expand in '49. Our basement wasn't big enough. I bought up half the block, and we broke through the walls of a drugstore, a Chinese delicatessen, and a moviehouse. I had close to five hundred clerks. Powder Burns kept shrinking our "slippage." He brought a touch of G-2 into Karp & Co., gathered his files in the basement, called a tiny room near the toilets his headquarters. I never visited him. I kept to the fifth floor, near my bay window with its panoramic view of the park. I'd go up to the roof with Willie and glimpse at the Hudson, remembering the mothballed ships that had sat in the mouth of the harbor only a couple of years ago.

Roz summoned me while I was still up on the roof.

"Mr. Kahn, your security man would like to see you."

"Christ," I said, "I'm sunbathing."

"In February?" she asked in her spinster's singsong voice.

"Tell Powder Burns to come up to the roof."

"He wants you in the basement, Mr. Kahn. He says it's urgent. A matter of life and death."

"Life and death," I muttered as I marched down the crumbling steps of Karp & Co. with Willie's tail beating against the banisters. I had the same old vertigo in my bargain basement. I'd sack Powder Burns if he ever interfered with my sunbathing again.

I found him in his tiny room, with the toilets hissing on the other side of the wall.

"Where's life or . . ."

A woman with a filthy face was sitting on the floor. Her hair was tangled in knots. She had pathetic summer shoes,

Salvation Army slacks, an old Eisenhower jacket ripped at the sleeves, a man's tie that served as a kind of scarf.

"She wasn't stealing, sir. She was huddling near the pipes. I didn't . . ."

"Get the hell out of here."

He hopped out of his headquarters, shrugging to himself, but I could have kissed my security chief. Fate had been kind to me all of a sudden. If I hadn't hired Powder Burns, I might never have found Red. I wasn't blind. I *knew* the shape of her under that filth. But I had to be careful. Karp & Co. wasn't the ETO.

The pup went out of his mind. He slobbered all over the rag lady. His pink eyes turned blood red. He couldn't have been a facsimile. Margaret rubbed his ears, like he was an old friend from the same battle zone. She didn't even question why or how Willie was with me in Manhattan.

"Roland," she said, "give me a drink."

My heart exploded after hearing her husky voice. I'd close the basement, declare a holiday if I had to.

"Let me take you upstairs, Red. To my office."

"You'll look gallant walking with me. I haven't bathed in a week."

"Sit there, please."

I jumped out, plucked a cashmere coat from one of the clothing barrels, put it around Red. My vertigo was gone. I'd live in a cellar if that's what she wanted.

I walked back up the creaking stairs with Willie and Red. Roz didn't say a word. I locked the door, took a towel from the president's washroom, soaked it in hot water, and returned to Red. My hand was shaking.

"If you cry, Roland, I'll kill you."

"Won't cry," I promised, but the tears wouldn't stop. It was Red who ended up washing my face. She was my own rag lady, and I wouldn't have altered her outfit for all the millions that Karp & Co. could bring. Her tattered remnants could have been the rotting uniform of a doughnut girl. The war had gone on and on and on for Red and me.

"I'm living with a man," she said.

I ordered a feast from Lüchow's, while Red sponged herself. She came out of the washroom bright and beautiful in her rags. She rearranged her hair, untangled the knots. Our feast arrived. She ate like a lion.

"I'm living with a man."

I was completely taken over by her appetite.

"How's baby Jon?" she asked.

"Who told you I had a son? Was it Powder Burns?"

"No. I'm a good Wellesley girl. I read the social pages of the *Times*. You're always attending galas."

"That's the businessman's curse."

"Don't complain. I couldn't have followed your career. You look cute in white tie and tails. I shouldn't have come here. I was resting, Roland. How could I have known that the phantom of G-2 was working in your store?"

"What about Wellesley? I tried . . ."

"Wellesley girls aren't human. They're crusaders and soldierettes with one mission. To change the world. I delivered doughnuts, sang to wounded GIs. That was easy. But I couldn't be a doughnut girl for the rest of my life. I never had that much attention."

"You're like me," I said.

"Certainly. The captain and his Red Cross moll . . . I have to go. And please don't stop me. I'll scratch your secretary's eyes out. I'm living with a man."

I wanted to imprison Red, keep her in my office, but I couldn't. She would have turned inward, stopped talking, hated me. I could feel the doom climb on my shoulder the minute she left, like a monkey on my back. Willie watched her with his pink eyes, and didn't even bump me with his nose. That's how miserable he was. He had his own little monkey on his back.

7

I should have returned to my own hearth, grown old with baby Jon and my darling wife, who was on the board of Karp & Co. and let me follow my own desires with our flagship on Union Square. But I heard a siren calling me. Could it have been Loreleis from the Rhine beckoning me back to Germany . . . and the doughnut truck I'd shared with Red?

I didn't wait for Bookie. I went up to Harlem, visited him in his offices at the Theresa Hotel, the black Waldorf-Astoria at Seventh Avenue and 125th Street. The black Waldorf had staircases that crumbled worse than Karp's. Bookie's suite on the ninth floor was flanked by a barber and a fortune-teller, both of whom belonged to Bookie and were part of his enterprises. I did retail, and Bookie was a wholesaler who supplied services and goods. I couldn't waltz into his suite. It had a steel door with a judas window, and the door was locked. I rapped on the steel plate with my knuckles and announced myself. "Roland Kahn."

The judas window slid open, and an eye peered at me.

"Brother, you must want the shylock down the hall. We ain't familiar with the Rolands and the Kahns."

"Just tell Bookie it's Captain Kidd."

The steel door opened with the clack of a hammer. I walked into Booker Bell Management Services, met colored men who gripped my hand, plied me with cigars, flutes of champagne, and a flower for my lapel until their boss could see me. And I had the damnedest surprise in Bookie's back office. It was like a homecoming party. There was Mordecai Jones, Josh Hill, and Zeke Hammer, and a couple of others from my old squad of MPs, laughing and hollering with Romulus Rivers Bell, who seemed to have grown since he left the academy. He had the beginnings of a mustache. He wore a sharkskin suit, like his dad. There was no mercy in his eyes for the clothing king.

He didn't dance with me, like the others did. The little general kept his distance. I was guilty as hell. I'd stolen whatever career he might have had at the academy, condemned him into becoming a gangster man.

My partner saw the monkey on my back. He knew I wouldn't have come up to Harlem on a whim. He dismissed his gang, ordered out his own son and my squad of MPs.

"Booker, you could have told me that Mordecai was at the Theresa. I would . . ."

"Little man, uptown and downtown don't mix."

"They did in the Third Army."

"No," Bookie said. "That was your delusion, and I went along."

"Didn't the MPs go to church with the Green Hornet?"

"He went to church with Willie, but that didn't make the

pup a soldier boy. . . . You saw Red, didn't you? I can tell that crazy look in your eye."

"It was a miracle. She was skulking around in the basement, trying to warm herself, dressed in rags, and Powder Burns got hold of her."

"I knew we shouldn't have hired him."

"What do you mean? He gets a bonus, bigger than—"

"And where is your doughnut girl?"

"That's the problem. She disappeared. You have to bring her back."

"No," Bookie said.

"Brother, if you won't help me, I'll have to spend my whole life with a monkey on my back."

She was living with Mario English in a cold-water flat. I never liked Mario, a fat man who drank his way out of a job with *Time* magazine. Mario was writing a novel. He couldn't support Red and himself with the meager advance he got from a Manhattan publisher. Of all the men in the world, why had she picked Mario? Had she taken pity on the fat son of a bitch? Booker got to him in two days.

"I'd suggest throwing him out the window. Mordecai will do it for free."

"No violence," I said. "You'll make a martyr out of him. And Red will love that fat man from the grave."

"Then we'll give him a scholarship to go to Chicago . . . without Red."

"Suppose he runs with Red and the money?"

"Little man, do I look like a fool? Mario goes my way, or he doesn't go at all."

"But if he loves her, Bookie, he'll refuse your proposition."

"We'll see."

Mario got on the night train to Chicago all by himself, as my partner had predicted. It didn't feel like a victory. It felt like a thief's answer to a thief's problem. I didn't want Red returned with some ruse.

I marked time, bit my knuckles, waited a week, and visited Red at her cold-water flat. It was on upper Fifth Avenue, at the edge of Harlem, along the railroad tracks. I didn't bring her flowers. I wasn't courting Red. I wanted to confess. I found her on the floor in some kind of delirium. I understood things better when I noticed the empty icebox and the empty shelves. I ran downstairs to the grocer, grabbed whatever I could buy. I fixed her some scrambled eggs, forced her to chew. The flat was freezing. I bundled her up in my own winter coat. She opened one eye and smiled. "Captain Kidd."

"Hey," I said, "what happened to that cashmere coat I got for you at Karp's?"

"I gave it to Mario."

"You had to fall in love with a novelist? They're all hunger artists. They think only of themselves."

"I'm not in love with Mario."

"But you were living with him. Didn't you tell me that three times? 'I'm living with a man.' "

"I wanted to throw you off the scent. Wellesley girls aren't homebreakers."

I shook her, very lightly. "Margaret, you're not at Wellesley anymore. . . . I bribed your fat man, sent him to Chicago to finish his novel."

"Bookie bribed him. He wouldn't have taken your money. He hates your guts."

"I can send you to Chicago . . . if you want."

"Keep talking," she said, "and I may fall in love with the fat man, just to spite you."

I stayed with Red, nursed her as much as I could. We didn't talk about the ETO, or her novelist. We didn't mention the Green Hornet once, though he could have been in that cold-water flat with us; that's how thick a slice of our past he commanded. I neglected Karp & Co. I neglected Lizabeth and our son. I came home at night, that's all. I had my dinners with Red. She wouldn't move out of the flat. I had the electricity turned on, and we didn't have to use candles all the time. And then, in the middle of a conversation, we started to kiss. Her freckles had always excited me. But I'm not talking passion. I'm not talking concubines on upper Park Avenue. I'm talking love. I could rest within the perfume of her spotted skin. I could lie down with her the whole afternoon.

"You're ruining your life, Captain Kidd. Your son will despise you when he grows up. I'm a nuisance to every man. Mario couldn't work while I was around. I had to sit in coffee shops."

"I'm not Mario."

We'd walk down to the Metropolitan, look at the Rembrandts, catch a foreign film at the Paris theatre. Was it *Devil in the Flesh* with Gérard Philipe? Or *The Walls of Malapaga* with Jean Gabin? We harmed no one. We ate at one of the French bistros on Ninth Avenue. I never brought her to Lüchow's, never flaunted Red in front of my employees. But my mom, Anna Karp, decided to steal my joy. She called a board meeting of Karp & Co. I was president, but Mom was chairman of a board filled with my own relatives. *She* sat at the head of the table, not Captain Kidd.

"We have to expand," Mom said. "It's grow or die. That's the modern world."

"Madam Chairman, I disagree. We have our market . . . at Union Square. We can outdraw Macy's and Gimbel's, but on our own turf. If you're considering a move uptown . . ."

"Not uptown, Mr. President. I'd like to open another store in Manhasset, at a shopping mall we happen to own. Think of it as a satellite."

"A bargain basement won't work in Manhasset, Mom."

"We have to push into the suburbs. We have to make the leap."

I was outvoted. Lizabeth remained loyal to me, but my dad didn't. I should have resigned. I could have gone wholesale, joined Bookie's gang. But I didn't have the little general's morbid charm. I couldn't play the blue-eyed Gypsy. I was Captain Kidd.

I cornered Mom after the meeting. The Karps had come from Upper Silesia. They were half Polish and had much more imagination that the Kahns, Jewish barons from Saxony.

"Your father traveled," Mom said.

"What?"

"He strayed from home. When it got serious, I bankrupted him and his mistress. He returned to Kahn & Kahn."

"Then it's all out in the open, huh? You've had me followed."

"No, my precious son. When you walk into the Metropolitan Museum of Art with a redheaded woman who isn't your wife, I'm bound to hear of it. I'm on the museum's board. So are you. But you never attend meetings. I could have your redhead arrested for vagrancy. But you're stubborn and volatile, a war hero. Your wife is beautiful, or did you forget? If she leaves you, Roland, I'll lose my only grandchild."

"Mom, I wouldn't hurt baby Jon."

"You might. You have a redhead on your mind."

"And so I'm banished to Siberia."

"Manhasset," said the chairman of the board. "You'll buy for both stores. You're president of Karp & Co. I've never told you how or what to sell. And you'll make a settlement with your redhead, a lifetime allowance, which we'll charge to Karp & Co."

"No settlements," I screamed. "No allowances. You hear me, Mom?" And I walked out of the boardroom, which was located on the top floor of Kahn & Kahn.

But I couldn't compete with Anna Karp's Silesian tactics. I wasn't the Green Hornet. I was an ex-captain who had to supervise the opening of a satellite. I didn't care about shopping patterns in the suburbs. I turned the entire store into a bargain basement. It was a monster success. But I had to abandon Red for weeks at a time, and Booker couldn't supply *two* bargain basements on his own. He had to call on other Harlem gangs.

"We'll lose our independence, little man."

"Bookie, I don't have a choice. My own board demanded another store."

"But I told you. When you rob from Macy's, you rob soft. And now we can't."

I returned to Red. We didn't go to museums. We kept away from the midtown landed gentry. We ate at home and sneaked into the Paris whenever we could, kissed in front of Gérard Philipe, or ventured into Harlem and danced at the Savoy.

We were safe on Lenox Avenue. After the riots of '43, when a white cop shot a black soldier and hell broke out in Harlem, Manhattan bluebloods wouldn't stroll uptown, not even to hear hot music at the Savoy. Lana Turner had danced there once upon a time. So did Garbo and Dietrich and the Duchess of Windsor. But we didn't find any movie stars or princesses in 1949. We had Harlem to ourselves. I'd stumble around on the Savoy's maple floor, while Red laughed at her dancing pirate, and we both marveled at a ballroom that had two bandstands and a soda fountain instead of a bar, with blue candles and a special milk shake called the Golden Goose, made with caramel, mint chocolate, and gobs of mocha ice cream. It was almost two feet high, and I developed an addiction for it. I'd sip my Golden Goose in front of the blue candles.

"Red, Red, couldn't we run away?"

She didn't even bother to answer. But I felt at peace clutching her hand in the dark of a dance hall. I could float into her body, dream. There was no other paradise for Captain Kidd. Mocha and caramel in my mouth and a candle on her face was all I'd ever need.

But I should have been wary of candles. Candles can cause a fire. I had a visitor at my office on Union Square, a plainclothesman from the Harlem precinct. He shouldn't have been able to reach downtown. His name was Daniel Beard. He banged through our basement, ran up a bill of three thousand dollars.

Willie growled at him. I had to restrain the pup. He would have torn off the policeman's toes. Beard wouldn't talk until I banished the pup to a dusty corner under my desk.

"Kahn, I'd like to open a charge account . . . in your name."

"Ah, then I owe you something, Officer Beard."

"Your health. Your cash flow. Insurance against a burning basement."

"And you can provide all that?"

"Of course. A full-proof policy."

"And the insurer is Daniel Beard?"

"No, Kahn. I work for the Milkman. Just ask Bookie about him."

I called Bookie in Harlem. "Who's the Milkman?"

"What happened?"

"A cop just shook me down. A white cop from Harlem."

"With a tick in one eye? Dan Beard. He collects for the

Milkman. . . . I told you not to mess with two stores. The Milkman's my competitor. I had to dip into his stock to keep our barrels full. And now he's asking for satisfaction. But it ain't like him to send Dan Beard. He would have visited you himself. I'll set it right."

Bookie must have had his mojo working. Because the Milkman did visit me the next afternoon. He came with Officer Beard, who returned the goods he'd swiped from Karp's. The cop had two swollen eyes. The Milkman was wearing a white turtleneck and a mink coat. He noticed the pup between my legs. I still couldn't place him, even after he saluted Willie and me.

"Staff Sergeant Michael Muldoon reporting to the captain, sir. . . . Didn't I spot Powder Burns in the basement, or was it a mirage?"

"You were in the Third Army?"

"With a colored tank battalion. We rolled right into Buchenwald. I couldn't sleep for a month. There were boxes and boxes of jewelry and gold teeth. I saw a man so thin, I could have folded him up like a chair. I had to feed him milk with a spoon. . . . But you left us early, Captain Kidd. Do you know why Booker and me have kicked all the other colored kings out of the Valley? Because they never went to school with the Green Hornet. They sat out the war. A white man comes marching, they run for cover. Not Booker, not me. We own the Valley, and soon we'll own Sugar Hill."

"Then I suppose you're partners with my partner."

"Harlem don't work that way. It's too unstable. If I had my own nigger tank battalion, I might make it work. Fact is, you'll have to choose between Booker and me. I'm patient. I wouldn't muscle in on a man. I'll give you a couple days. But you'll get much better value with the Milkman. I have a bigger, meaner machine. I can promise you half of Macy's."

"I served with Booker, and most of his gang."

"Captain, ain't you been listening? You also served with me."

I couldn't do anything but sit while the war began. Officer Beard was the first victim. He was found frozen in the middle of an ice block. I had lunch with Booker at Lüchow's. He didn't come alone. He had bodyguards, retired detectives from the homicide squad.

"Bookie, you can't turn a white cop into an icicle, not in this town. People start to notice."

"I didn't touch Dan Beard. The Milkman did. He couldn't forgive him for trying to hustle you on his own."

"Then why'd you bring bodyguards along?"

"Because the Milkman is planning to cut my throat. He wants to grab up Karp's account. He tried to smoke Romulus twice. My kid had to step out of a perilous fire to stay alive. The Milkman knows about Red. He could burn all her hair . . . and kidnap the pup."

I ran uptown with Willie. "You can't live here," I told Red. "The Milkman is on the warpath. He's a murderer and a thief."

Willie couldn't stop slobbering. I had to slap him on the butt, or he would have ruined Red's floor.

I brought Red and her clothes down to Karp & Co., installed her in my office.

"What will I do here?"

"I'll build you into the company, make you a junior partner."

"Roland, I've never been anything but a doughnut girl."

"You've read Shakespeare and Molière. You've studied the misfortunes of life. You can shape new policies for us."

"How?" she asked. "As Roland Karp's whore? I'll sell for you, walk the floors, like your other clerks."

It was a harrowing week. Red wasn't used to the hurly-burly of a paying job. She couldn't roam in a German forest, give out woolen socks to GIs. She had to sell girdles in a basement that was like an enormous bomb shelter. All the bartering confused her, the exchange of goods for crumpled green bills. She wanted to give all the goods away. The other clerks grew jealous. They'd never seen me in the basement so much. I would assist Red, ease her nerves with a customer, simplify a sale.

My mother marched into the store. I caught her looking at Red, but she wouldn't have wrinkled her nose at a Wellesley girl. Mom was much too aristocratic and clever. I had to follow her up to the president's office. She ignored Willie, puttered around among Red's things, absorbed in the material like a good merchant.

"You'll fire her, this instant. I'll get her a job at Saks."

Imbecile that I was, I'd never realized the resemblance between Mom and Red. Both had a shy, hysterical beauty, but Mom's was covered up with a hundred years of mercantilism, the special patina of the Karps.

"Mom, she stays with me. I don't have a choice. There's trouble on the streets."

"You can't *live* with her at Karp's. We'll be laughed at. I won't be able to lunch at a decent place."

"Blame it on Manhasset, Mom."

"I forbid you to talk riddles to your own mother."

"I couldn't fill two bargain basements. The turnover was tumultuous. We had to borrow from here and there."

"You mean . . ."

"We steal from Macy's and Gimbel's. I had to go into business with thieves."

She summoned her board. The president of Karp & Co. was locked out of the meeting. I didn't cry. After Mom's people huddled for five hours, I was called in. Lizabeth wasn't with the board. Mom had decided to distance her from my own dirty deeds.

"Dad," I said, "have we had a profitable year?"

"Very."

"And what would we have had without my own creative resources?"

"A catastrophe."

"Then either get a new president, or don't interfere."

"The stores can't survive without you, son . . . but we could shut down the Manhasset branch."

"It's too late," I said. "We're in the middle of a war."

I returned to Red. We had champagne. I'd kicked Roz

out of her office, attached it to mine, and we had our own little suite . . . with Willie the warrior. Red would have sent me back to Fifth Avenue and baby Jon in the middle of the night, but she was still too jumpy about her job. My soldier's body must have soothed her. I dreamt of Willie, saw him sitting near the Old Man's trunk, waiting for a general who would never reappear. And I sensed in the thick of sleep that it was a miserable omen, that I'd have to pay a price for dreaming of that dog who was snoring right near Red.

Booker woke me. It was four A.M. He'd burgled his way into Karp & Co. He said hello to Red and the pup, then squinted in my direction.

"Rollie, the Milkman came down Fifth Avenue tonight, kidnapped baby Jon."

My partner had to dress me. I couldn't get my own buttons to meet. That's how much of a pirate I was. Captain Kidd.

8

• Lizabeth didn't scold. She was deep in shock, while detectives bounced all over the apartment, hunting for clues. Neighbors arrived in bathrobes, talked about the three masked men who broke into the building.

"Never saw such masks on a man. Paper bags with eyeholes, like a child would wear. But these weren't children."

The bulls left at six in the morning. I told them nothing about the Milkman. Mom appeared with a nightgown under her mink coat. I must have been in a trance, because she looked like a teenaged girl in the dim light, a lost Ophelia. She slapped my face.

"Is this how you conduct business?"

"It's war, Mom. What could I do? I'll find the baby."

"Baby? He's almost three. He eats like a little gentleman. He talks like a philosopher. But a libertine like you, a man who chases lollipops, would never bother to notice."

She started to pull my hair. It hurt. But I couldn't pluck at my own mother. It would have been like incest.

"My good-for-nothing war hero who brings gangsters into the firm."

Mom's screams brought Lizabeth out of shock. She appeared in her own nightgown, shook Mom's shoulder.

"Anna, you'll pull out all his hair."

"He deserves it. Let him do his penance as a bald man."

"I don't want penance," Lizabeth said. "I want my husband alive."

"So he can go to parties with his lollipop?"

Lizabeth looked into Mom's eyes. It chilled me. They were like *two* Ophelias. "Anna, if my husband has a lollipop, it concerns him, not you."

"Lizabeth," I muttered. I was crying now. "I'll bring the baby back, I promise."

"Wait," my wife said. She kissed me, caressed my scalp, collected the clumps of hair Mom had torn from my head. I was Roland Kahn, the errant jack of hearts.

I took a cab to the Theresa Hotel, knocked on Booker's steel door. "Captain Kidd."

I was allowed into the war room. The whole gang was there, with pistols strapped to their shoulders. Romulus had inherited the Green Hornet's pearl-handled Colt. Had I given it to him? I hated guns. What kind of officer had I been? Had I really rolled with George? A tanker who'd never been inside a tank.

"I'm heading the team," I said. "I still outrank everybody in the room."

"If you don't keep quiet, we'll put you in a corner, Captain Kidd."

"For God's sake, have you made contact with the Milkman?"

"Contact? Harlem's his crib. Not even the Third Army could find him if he didn't want to get found."

"But isn't the Theresa also Harlem?"

"Tell him, Ezekiel."

"When a brother be hiding, he stay hid. Harlem is the land of missing persons."

"But my son is inside that land, Zeke."

"That's the sadness of it," said my old MP.

"And why is Romulus wearing the Green Hornet's gun? It's sacrilege, Booker. He was with the commandos. He was on Hitler's side."

"Rollie, you left the Hornet's gun with me. And I have jurisdiction over who wears it and who don't. And we already settled the question about what my kid was doing outside the castle."

"He was going to lead us into a death trap."

"But he didn't. We were the first Americans he ever saw. The heinies had told him stories. He was expecting cruel devils, and we came along. A skinny captain acting like a chauffeur for a white pup and a colored MP. He adopted us from that moment on."

"And you believe that tale?"

"Brother Rollie, don't be calling Bookie's boy a liar in our own war room."

"All right," I said. "I'll apologize in the name of the pup."

"Dad," Romulus said. "I want more than that from Uncle Rollie."

"I'm not your uncle, and I never was."

The kid smiled. He was closing in on sixteen. "You're

my second dad. That's what it says in the books. And you're worse to me than a stranger."

I was. I hadn't given up my old animus against him. I still wanted to strangle Romulus Rivers Bell.

There was a gun battle on St. Nicholas Avenue that same afternoon. Zeke was killed. The cops didn't even connect it to the kidnapping.

"Let them murder themselves," said the midtown detective who'd inherited my son's case. "Our kidnappers are definitely white."

"How can you be so sure?" I asked Detective Samuel Snipes, who'd found the Constantine baby, scion of a Manhattan millionaire. Snipes had traced the kidnapper through a ransom note. The penmanship had been a little too perfect. The culprit had come out of a reform school where *f*'s and *g*'s had to be looped in a particular way. Snipes went through the reform school's records and captured him in a week.

"Listen to me. No shine would ever dare invade Fifth Avenue. It's an unwritten law. We'll catch the bastards soon as there's a ransom note."

But there never was a note. The Milkman's message was clear. If I agreed to forsake Bookie and my other blood brothers, I could get Jonathan back. I was tempted to sell out everyone I knew, but then I thought of the Green Hornet's aristocratic lines. "Rollie," he'd say, "birth is your only station." That's why the Hornet took to Captain Kahn. I was his "Hebrew aristocrat." And even if I'd wanted to deal, in spite of George, I had no means of communicating with the Milkman.

Two of my other MPs were shot in the street. Romulus Rivers Bell was losing an uncle every other day. I didn't go to work. I'd comfort Lizabeth, feed her hot milk, swear I'd bring Jonathan back, and then go out looking for the scion of Karp & Co. I went as far as I could into the land of missing persons, with Willie at my heels. No one harmed me. I sang my name—"Captain Kidd"—and colored people shook my hand.

"Ain't you Third Army? Didn't you lead a black brigade? You're with the Booker Bell mob."

I didn't go to rent parties. I didn't go slumming at the Savoy. I was too damned guilty to hop around with Red. I tied Willie to a lamppost and drank ordinary milkshakes at a soda fountain on Lenox Avenue that was a world of mirrors. I could catch my own image a thousand times with each sip. That fountain was called the Little Savoy, because it was near the big ballroom, and it became my headquarters in Harlem. I had to find a place that wasn't too populated if I wanted the Milkman to contact me. I sat and waited, wondered what messenger the Milkman would choose. A white cop, like Dan Beard? But Dan was already dead. A high yellow girl? Or the Milkman himself?

Then I realized what a genius he was, a genuine tanker. Only the Green Hornet could have trained him. A little boy entered that world of mirrors, traveled across an infinite road of glass, and stopped at my table. The jack of hearts didn't even recognize his own son. Jonathan couldn't have grown like that. But I hadn't been around him in months.

"Papa," he said, tugging at my pants. Where did he find his vocabulary?

"Would you like a soda, son?"

"Papa, I promised the Milkman. Come."

It was miraculous. Sentences grew out of him like trees. He gripped my hand. I paid the bill. We got into a Packard outside the Little Savoy with Willie the warrior. A man put a paper bag over my head. Without eyeholes. But at least George had taught me about terrain. I knew we'd climb and climb into Sugar Hill . . .

We got out of the car, with Jon holding my hand, leading me along, Willie behind us. We entered an elevator, climbed again, arrived at a landing, crept along a hallway. A door closed behind me. Someone pulled off the paper bag. We were in a huge apartment that overlooked a park.

The Milkman sat on a couch. My own son jumped into his lap.

"You've got a way with kids," I told the Milkman.

"He misses his mom, but it's better than nursery school."

"He doesn't go to school. He's a baby."

"Wanna bet?"

"Milkman, you could go to the electric chair."

"And you can go to the devil if I don't get what's coming to me. A full partnership, Captain. I'm desperate. My money's drying up."

"And if I refuse?"

"I'll smoke you and your kid."

I expected Willie to jump on the Milkman, tear out his

throat, but when he heard the Milkman bark, he ran under the sofa, like a brilliant attack dog.

"Milkman, look at me. Jon loves you. You're his nurse."

"Told you. I'm desperate."

There was a rumble at the door. Two of the Milkman's lieutenants arrived with Romulus Rivers Bell. His ear was bleeding.

"Look what what we found, Mr. Muldoon. Booker's rat boy."

I rolled my eyes. "Rom, what the hell are you doing up here?"

"Shadowing you, Captain Kidd."

"I don't need shadowing. I was about to negotiate a deal."

"With the Milkman? He killed three of my uncles."

The taller lieutenant handed the Milkman my antique Colt. "The rat boy was carrying this."

"Love a duck," the Milkman said, twirling my Colt. "Captain, ain't that the Green Hornet's gun?"

"Mr. Muldoon," the shorter lieutenant asked, "what should we do with the rat boy?"

"I don't care. Smoke him. Kiss him. But get him out of my sight."

He couldn't stop twirling the gun. That was his *faiblesse*. He shouldn't have been concentrating on the Green Hornet with that little assassin in the house. Rom moved like an electrical storm, grabbed the gun away, shot the tall lieutenant and the short, killed them both in an instant. But he wanted the Milkman to die slow. He shot him in the groin, and then

I leaped in front of the Milkman, while baby Jon stared at the wonder of it all and the pup whimpered under the sofa.

"You can't kill him. He rolled with George. He's a Third Army man."

"He could be lying. Should I tell you how many clowns I met who talk tanks?"

"Milkman," I muttered, "start singing for your life. Convince this kid."

"I can't," the Milkman said. "I'm suffering too much."

I didn't like the way Rom was clutching that Colt. I panicked. Who knows how long he'd been killing people? He could have shot baby Jon for the fun of it. I grabbed Jon, shoved him behind me. The kid took advantage of my hysteria to shoot the Milkman in the hip.

"Sing, I said!"

"I can't . . . but I'll tell you, Captain. I was with the Hornet after the war. We rolled into Bavaria . . . right behind the doughnut girls."

My hand shivered. The son of a bitch knew how to gnaw at me.

"The girls hadn't been shipped home?"

"They stuck with the Hornet, through thick and thin."

"And the redheaded one?"

"She was his favorite, Captain. She danced with George."

I could feel the bullet in my own groin. My sweetheart's history began to make sense. She'd never recovered from George. That's why she'd settled for that fat novelist. As consolation.

100

I knocked the Colt out of Romulus' hand. "Get out of here."

"With my gun."

"Go!"

I called my savior, Detective Snipes. Told him that I'd found Jon with the help of a Third Army man, Sergeant Michael Muldoon.

The Milkman was rushed to the hospital, but he was never charged with any crime. Snipes realized that Muldoon was the third kidnapper, but he couldn't risk calling me a liar. I was the war hero, not him. I coached baby Jon. He wouldn't give the Milkman away.

"Bullets," he said. "Bang bang."

Willie and I looked for Red. She'd removed her clothes from our little suite at Karp & Co., returned to upper Park Avenue. She hadn't quit her job. She still clerked in the basement. But she'd gone absent without leave. I went up to her cold-water flat. She wasn't there. I shook with terror, and then I had a thought. *Danced with George.* Where would she go to recall Germany and the war? I floated up to the Savoy, did my own little cakewalk with Willie. I could barely get in. They didn't like having bull terriers in a ballroom. I had to leave Willie with the hatcheck girl. He looked at me with his pink eyes. I'd disappointed the pup.

Red wasn't out on the floor. It was packed with hot mamas who must have done the lindy every night of the week. There were a few soldiers and sailors, white and black, and

I figured Red might have been lindying with them. But she would have done a slow dance with George. . . .

There was the usual battle of the bands, with a black trombone and his men on the number-one bandstand, and a white hunchback saxophone at the other end of the hall. The hunchback couldn't even start to blow. He was waiting for the trombone to finish his set. The dancers were wild about Harry the Cat. They wouldn't let him off the floor. Then their fury subsided a bit. The trombone mopped his forehead and sank into the little cozy hell of the Savoy's collapsible stage.

The dancers quit the floor. They weren't much interested in a white hunchback. And that's when I noticed Red. She was at the Savoy's soda fountain, eating a Golden Goose.

No one bothered you at the Savoy if you didn't want to be bothered. There were bouncers everywhere. Red sat alone, on her stool. I went up to her. One of the black bouncers glared at me. He'd become Margaret's protector. But he stopped scowling when Red started to talk.

"Who told you to come here? I'm not your little article, Captain Kidd."

"Dance with me."

"The floor was red hot, and now it's cold. That hunchback is from hunger. He has two left hands."

"I don't care."

The hunchback tootled a bit. He was warming up, a one-man band. He leaned back on his heels and started to blow. There was a stab of pain that shot up from the roots of my legs. He had my melody, plaintive and slow.

"That's Bones McHenry," she said. "I heard him play

before the war. He's from Minneapolis . . . like me."

Red could say what she wanted. I liked Bones. He didn't pretend to be a black orchestra. He stood on his tiny bandstand, a corner with a rope in front of it, and played "My Heart's on Fire." I couldn't really tell the difference between hot and cold. I was no jazzman. I'd never done the lindy in my life. I could trot around like a crippled toad. And Bones McHenry was the musician for me.

I danced with Red to the hunchback's slow designs. We were stranded on that maple floor where you could watch your own shadow in the polished wood. But I was watching Red. Someone bumped me. It was William the Conqueror. He must have escaped from the hatcheck room. He was following our steps on the floor while he nuzzled my girl. I ignored him, whispered in Red's ear.

"You couldn't start your life . . . now I get it."

"Roland, are you dancing or mumbling?"

"You stayed with the Old Man. . . . You were with him in Bavaria."

"I was a doughnut girl attached to the Third Army."

"But you didn't go home, like I did. You danced with George."

"Yes."

"You loved him."

"All the girls did."

"But he only danced with you . . ."

"Is the interrogation over, Captain Kidd?" She started to cry. "I didn't give a damn about anything except doughnuts and Willie and George . . . and you. But you were gone."

Bones McHenry swiveled his hips. The chandeliers seemed to rock with his sad wailing. People were coming out onto the floor. They couldn't do the lindy. But they were learning to appreciate a hunchback who didn't have his own disappearing bandstand. They bent lower and lower to his melancholy beat. Their heads were near the floor. I could see their faces in the wax. Bones had gotten to them, Bones was entering their blood. It was the strangest fox-trot, men and women struggling against a single saxophone. I didn't dream of the future while the hunchback wailed. I didn't even dream of George. I had Red in my arms. That was enough. Willie bumped me again and again, his pink eyes burning in the dark. "Cut it out," I warned him. But the pup was part of our dance.

RED

9

• Georgie was so proud. He was the first of Ike's generals to piss in the Rhine. Margaret hadn't watched him pee. But she could imagine the Green Hornet with his fly unbuttoned, screaming "Hot dog!" Ike wouldn't let him piss in the Moldau and take Prague. And pretty soon there were no more rivers, no more towns to take. Georgie Patton had to sit behind a desk. "Margaret," he'd whisper, "I should have been killed by the last bullet of the war. Then I could rest in Valhalla."

"With Caesar's ghost."

It was June '45. He was head of an occupation army, the military governor of Bavaria, but he didn't know how to govern. "I'm a housekeeper," Georgie would groan. Bavaria was filled with homeless people, who'd wander about the countryside searching for firewood, a roof, bits of sugar. There was no electricity, no mail, no running water. The Third Army had its own train, with Georgie's private car, but no civilian could travel on a military railroad. The bitterness would return soon as he stopped laughing. "If Ike had let me take the big casino, we wouldn't have all the Mongols on our back."

He blamed the Russians, the Gypsies, the Jews. German officers were part of his special priesthood: men who trained other men to kill. And Georgie's own priesthood was disintegrating. "It's like leprosy," he said of the Third Army. "I'm losing a finger and a foot every day." Georgie's knights were itchy to go home.

Margaret and the other doughnut dollies had followed the general to his new headquarters, a nine-hundred-room building on forty acres at Bad Tölz, in the foothills of the Bavarian Alps. The building had once been an SS officers' training school. Margaret and the other girls called it The Mountain. They had their own little warren among the nine hundred rooms, but they were constantly getting lost. They had to carry whistles, or they wouldn't have found one another.

The dollies were as restless as Georgie's troops. They had boyfriends in Colorado, careers, or a marriage they intended to pursue. Margaret had nothing. She was a waif among waifs, with George and Willie.

The Old Man believed in reincarnation. He'd been to war with Caesar, had sat at bonfires with William the Conqueror, Willie's namesake. "Red, I was a soldier before I was seven."

He'd invite her to his "ranch," a villa on Lake Tegernsee, fifteen minutes from The Mountain. It had once belonged to the publisher of *Mein Kampf.* But the general didn't have much peace at his villa. Correspondents would pester him. They needed something sensational. They didn't have the war and Georgie's drives across Germany. Mario English was with them. He'd flutter his eyes at Red.

"Kay Summersby."

"Call me that again, and I'll strangle you."

He'd run behind the other war correspondents. "My sweet, darling little Kay."

The girls would razz her too. How could she fight their jealousy, even if she swore that she wasn't sleeping with the Green Hornet? Sergeants saluted her. MPs would let her in and out of any door. There was nothing Margaret could do about it. She'd become the general's lady.

She'd ride in Georgie's train. He'd gobble up his cigars and drink whiskey, but he wouldn't play poker with his staff, like other generals, or sneak German countesses into his car. He played casino with Margaret. It was his only vestige of war, building bundles, trying to capture aces. Sometimes, when that deep sadness crept into his eyes, she'd let the Green Hornet win. He'd wink at her, shout "Hot dog!"

He was as concentrated as a man moving a battalion of tanks. She could have been Rommel at the other side of the card table. But Rommel was dead. And she didn't have much use for reincarnation. She needed Rollie in this life, and she couldn't have him.

George wouldn't invite any of the correspondents onto the train. He didn't have to give interviews. But the correspondents would send her notes. "How's the general, Kay?"

And she'd glance at herself in the mirror, comb her red hair, and wonder what the real Kay Summersby looked like. She didn't have to wonder anymore. The supreme commander stopped the train outside Stuttgart and climbed aboard with his Scottie, Telek . . . and Kay Summersby. She'd driven Ike from Mannheim to meet the train. And Red lost her courage. She felt like a rag doll compared to that tall Irish beauty. Kay didn't have to deal with candy bars and coffee. She looked like a general in her uniform, not a doughnut girl. She wore a man's tie. But not even an imbecile from the forests could have mistaken her for a man. She didn't have four stars on her shoulder, like Ike, and she didn't need them. Her hair flamed much deeper than Red's. And she wasn't burdened with so many freckles.

Red was ruined in one glance. But she didn't have time to sulk. War broke out between Telek and Willie the Conqueror. The Green Hornet had banished Willie from his car while Telek was around. Telek sat in Willie's spot under the table, between everybody's legs. Telek didn't lick Kay Summersby's shoes, or put his nose near Red's ankles. He was a perfect gentleman, proud to be where he was. But Willie sneaked back into the car in the middle of lunch, behind one of the waiters. He had none of Telek's gallantry, or shrewdness about protocol. He went after Telek—and destroyed the meal Georgie's cook had prepared. The wine bottle flew into Red's lap. The table rocked, but no one could root out Willie and Telek. It was like a battle between the Third Army and SHAEF. The Green Hornet had to call in his MPs, who lifted the table. He cursed Willie. "Miserable mutt." His high-pitched howling couldn't do a thing. The mess boys tossed soapy water at the generals' dogs. Willie stopped fighting all of a sudden. He must have absorbed the listlessness of the Third Army, whose tankers could no longer roll, and he had to invent his own little war. He disappeared into the kitchen galley, Patton's last warrior.

The Hornet apologized. "Ike, it's awful. I have an ingrate on my staff . . . Sergeant Willie."

But Ike wasn't bothered at all. "This is Willie's home, George. We should lock up Telek."

"No, sir. Telek stays. He outranks Willie. And I'm glad you brought him. Willie's under arrest." And then the Hornet found his mettle. "Hot dog! Rank or no rank, Ike, my Willie was tearing the bejesus out of Telek."

"He was," Kay said, taking the wine bottle out of Red's lap. She had a whole world of music in her eyes. She spoke with a lilt that Margaret would never have. But she wasn't mocking Margaret. And she didn't have to fight under a table. Ike lacked the Hornet's charm. He was a slightly rumpled man who had a gift for juggling generals around. It was Kay who provided the melody to his life in the ETO. He wasn't a tanker. He'd never pissed in the Rhine.

George suggested a game of casino. He wanted to trap Ike, sting him where he could. But Margaret wasn't going to become George's bull terrier. She wouldn't build sensational bundles for *her* general. She shuffled the cards, that's it. Ike had all the aces.

"George, there are still Nazis in your sector."

"Ike," George said, holding a pair of cards over his eyes, like a dead man. "I have no electricity, no water. I'll root out the Nazis, but after I get this gawdamn country running again. I can't get rid of *all* the specialists on our team. We have a right to them. We won the war."

"General," Ike said, without raising his voice. "I expect every single Nazi or suspected Nazi removed from your headquarters tomorrow by thirteen hundred hours."

"Aw, Ike, I'll have to deliver candles to half the population."

"Then you'll deliver them. That's an order."

"Yes, sir," the Hornet said, removing the cards from his eyes. He hadn't swiped any bundles from the supreme commander. The visit was over. Kay shook Red's hand. "I'm glad we had a chance to meet. . . . The boys keep raving about you."

"Me? I'm a doughnut dolly."

"Who's been everywhere the troops have been."

"She's Third Army," the Hornet said, with his raspy voice. "And the best casino player in the world."

"Is that why you sat us down, George?" Kay said with a smile that broke the tension at the table. She got off the train with Telek and Ike.

"He'll never visit Third Army again," George groaned. "I'm the Green Hornet. I hit too hard. . . . The hell with Topside. Comes here with his dog and his whore."

"General, please stop that."

"Well, Kay's his redheaded bitch. Everybody knows that."

"And what am I, George?"

"You? You're Rollie's girl."

"And where is Rollie?"

"In Manhattan," the Hornet said.

"With his fiancée."

"Hot dog! I'll send out an expedition. We'll capture that ol' pirate. Bring him to Bavaria."

Margaret couldn't even laugh. Because there was a wisdom to what the Hornet had said. Rollie would have cured some of the general's ills. He wouldn't have let him rave about Nazis in front of Ike. He would have rehearsed the Hornet. But Rollie had to steal liebfraumilch and jeopardize his general, leave Margaret and Willie and the Hornet in a war zone without a war. She stopped loving him a little when she realized how reckless he'd been with other people's lives.

The Hornet went on leave in July, returned to the States to sell bonds for Uncle Sam and visit with his people. Margaret didn't like to talk about the Hornet's wife. Her name was Bea. He couldn't have survived all those years between two world wars without her. She was an heiress who'd gone to live in an army barracks with George. He would write poems to Bea. But he was nervous. The war had made him wild.

"I'll miss you, Red."

And she didn't know who the hell she was. A daughter manqué? Or a doughnut dolly who happened to be Roland's girl in one little corner of the ETO? She was like a spook without the general. She didn't know where to put herself, where to go. She could swim at the general's villa. No one questioned her movements. No one flirted with her except Mario English, and it was with half a heart. Mario was much too scared of the Hornet, whose power seemed to multiply the further he got from Bavaria.

She read about George's triumphs in America, where young girls and old, old men tossed flowers at him everywhere he went . . . and about his foibles, how he'd rage in the middle of a speech, shove his foot in his mouth one more time, and talk about soldiers who had died *foolishly*. Peace was much too prickly for the general. He didn't understand politics. He could only attack, push ahead. He should have been the commandant of Prague or Berlin. But he'd saved the Lipizzaner horses, kept them out of Russian hands. The Lipizzaners were the finest parade horses on the planet. There were about four centuries of training behind each horse. George had taken Red to Salzburg, where he rode a horse that Hitler had wanted to give to Emperor Hirohito. The horse was called Favory Africa. Margaret didn't know why. But she loved seeing her general on that white stallion, its hooves kicking the earth, as if horse and rider owned whatever territory they happened to be on. Did Favory Africa remind him of Alexander the Great? He seemed obsessed on the horse, his blue eyes sending him into other countries. He didn't need a modern war while he was on Favory Africa. He didn't need tanks. And for a moment he could forget Bad Tölz. . . .

She wandered in those nine hundred rooms, officers and dog soldiers saluting her. It was like the devil's own reincarnation. She was almost Patton while Patton was away. His staff didn't ask her to sit in the Hornet's chair, but she didn't have to. And it was while she was wandering that she saw a strange refugee who was as familiar to her as his own missing ear. He didn't have an American uniform at Bad Tölz. He wasn't playing Farnsworth, Bruce. And he wasn't a phantom. He was just another refugee, half-starved, looking for oranges and chicken bones.

She could have turned him in. The supreme commander might have given her a couple of gold stars. And she had no particular reason to be kind to an officer of the SS who'd pretended to be with German intelligence. Hadn't he tried to kill the Hornet?

"Hello," she said. "My darling Major Müller."

He refused to look at Margaret.

She gave him an apple and a chocolate bar out of her Red Cross kit.

He seized the apple, gnawed at it, his hands shaking. Then he sniffed at the chocolate, chewing with a cannibal hunger *and* disdain. "American chocolate," he said. "Freckles, have you ever tasted a Sacher torte?"

"What the heck is that?"

"A thin chocolate cake that was born at a hotel in Vienna."

"Vienna," she said. "Isn't that where the Lipizzaners come from?"

"Clever girl. The Lipizzaners' stables are right around the corner from that hotel. You shouldn't have shot my ear off."

"And you shouldn't have gone after the Green Hornet."

"That was my specialty. Kidnapping generals."

"And my specialty is giving SS officers to the provost marshal."

"No," Müller said. "You live with a general and feed doughnuts to his dog."

She could have walloped him, but Müller might have collapsed, and she would have been forced to hold him in her arms, rock the major. But soon she was sorry she hadn't socked him. Something fell out of his sleeve, glinted in the darkened halls of Bad Tölz. It was a spoon that Müller had sharpened and shaped into a knife. He scratched her throat with the spoon.

"Sacher torte," she mumbled. "Sacher torte."

"Fräulein Freckles, give me all you've got."

"Or what will you do? Bring in your comrades from Castle Höllenhund?"

"I'll slit your throat. I'm desperate. I have no comrades. I'm alone."

"And you happened to hitchhike to Bad Tölz. This was your training ground, wasn't it? This is where you went to school with the SS. It's the only goddamn place a killer could hide."

He scratched a little deeper with the spoon. But he couldn't seem to look into Margaret's eyes. "Müller, what's your Christian name?"

"Willy," he said, digging her into the wall. "Freckles, no one'll ever find you again."

A couple of MPs strolled by. She could have shouted, but she didn't. They saluted her, and tried not to notice the man in rags that Red was with. The MPs whistled their way into the darkness. Müller didn't even tremble. He had an assassin's touch. He meant to finish her. It would have been as natural to him as a yawn.

"Fräulein, you shouldn't have recognized me."

"And missed the pleasure of meeting an old acquaintance? Willy, I'm a sentimental gal."

One of her arms was still free, and she struck him on the side of the head with her kit. He tried to scoop her flesh away, cut her off at the neck, as if she were some hopeless lamb of a girl. But he couldn't slaughter Red just like that. She'd stepped outside the path of his spoon. She tripped him, and Red couldn't say what possessed her. She struck him again and again . . . until he was gone. He knew the perimeters of Bad Tölz, and Red didn't. She was lucky to turn the right corner in that nine-hundred-room affair.

Margaret no longer had the pocket pistol George had given her. She wandered around with a staple gun in her bag. She was prepared to staple Müller's head to the wall. But she never got the chance. He disappeared, like some cellar rat. She had to tell the provost's people about him. Müller might have menaced the other doughnut dollies. A hundred MPs combed The Mountain. But they couldn't capture one cellar rat with a missing ear. And Margaret was sort of glad. The dollies were safe with Müller on the run. And Margaret didn't mind having the major turn into something a little more mysterious than a ragged refugee.

10

• Time began to splinter into little useless pieces without the Hornet. Red and the other dollies fell into a dream. The Third Army was producing sleepwalkers. Red almost missed the romance of a knife in her neck. George was in Los Angeles. He telephoned Bad Tölz, talked to his chief of staff . . . and Margaret. He moaned at her.

"I'm dying."

"How's Willie?"

"Didn't you hear what I said?"

"General, we're dying without you too."

"It's not the same thing. You have tanks and flags and an officers' mess."

"None of us can eat in that mess without the Green Hornet."

"Red, you're coddling me. And I'm serious. I have to make speeches. I have to eat civilian grub. . . . How's my cook?"

"Dying without you, George."

"Shut up. I'm paying for this call, not you or General Eisenhower. Have you been on the bus?"

That's what he called the Third Army's locomotive. But how could Red ride on the Hornet's bus? "Where would I go, George?"

"To Africa . . . or Sicily."

"Has the bus become a submarine? Or are the army engineers building rails across the ocean?"

"Just climb on the bus, Red. And take a ride for ol' George. I'll dream about you. And I'll feel less lonely."

She couldn't figure out the Hornet. His simplest conversations were like tactical tricks. A doughnut dolly couldn't commandeer the Third Army train. The MPs would have arrested her for appropriating government property. And even if she played the pirate to please her general, who would have let her on board? She bowled at the Hornet's villa with five other dollies. She kept bumping into dog soldiers in the dark. She picked lice out of children's hair, fed refugees. The heat was unbearable in July. And like some saltimbanque, a sleepwalking clown, she rose off her bunk at Bad Tölz in the middle of the night, put on her uniform, walked to the depot, and climbed onto the bus. No one challenged her, not one cop. She didn't have to sit on a darkened train. A light turned on with the sound of a stinging bee in Georgie's private car. The whole bus was ablaze. She heard the tramp of dog soldiers as the train began to fill. The chief brakeman entered the car with the Hornet's aide-de-camp. Both men saluted her. She must have gotten them out of bed. Their eyes were bloodshot.

"Our destination, Lieutenant Young?"

119

What did George love to say? That battle plans would pop into his head like Minerva. He never had to think.

"Vienna," she spat at them. "Vienna."

"We'll have to notify the Russkies, Lieutenant, ma'am. Wouldn't want to start a war. We can't enter the Russian zone without some kind of signal or communiqué. What's the object of our mission?"

"Sacher torte," she said.

They saluted her again. "Sacher torte. Very good, Lieutenant, ma'am."

Nothing moved, nothing rolled for fifteen minutes. She read a battered copy of *Harper's Bazaar*. All the models were wearing uniforms. There was an interview with Marlene Dietrich, who was also in uniform. The theme of the issue was women at war. Margaret felt estranged from all the patriotic mumbo jumbo. She'd fed too many starving children to consider the role of women in the ETO. Now she understood the Hornet's dilemma in the States. They could lionize him in Los Angeles, but few of those civilians grasped the crazy dance of war. The Green Hornet went into battle with Hannibal at his side, "jumped off" with Caesar's ghost. And his dog, William the Conqueror, was as vital to him as his maps and his tank divisions.

The train started to lurch, and Red watched the Bavarian dawn. She began to feel guilty. She could have fed a thousand children with all the fuel this train was eating up. But she was Margaret Young, the saltimbanque, on her way to the land of Sacher tortes. There were no magic mountains in the mist. Only refugees beside the railroad tracks. And Red didn't have the power to offer them a ride on Georgie's train.

A kitchen boy brought her breakfast. She had eggs and buttered toast, like the Hornet, and a pot of black coffee. And that's when she fell out of the Third Army's broken dream of time. She could have been traveling for days, grown a man's beard. The countryside was in ruins. The train stopped. Margaret must have escaped Bavaria, entered the Russian zone, one more ruin. Russian officers climbed aboard and poked their heads into the Hornet's car, but they didn't ask to see any papers. They wore knee-high boots polished to perfection; the leather seemed to burn in the dim light, as if they'd come prancing out of a fire. They clicked their heels, saluted Margaret, called her *Madame Générale*. Then they jumped off the train with their burning boots.

Red rode into Austria. There were still refugees following the tracks. She had a luncheon of roast beef and liebfrau-milch. And she started to cry, thinking of Captain Kidd. "Madame Générale," she muttered. "You're a foolish girl. Romance doesn't have to begin and end with one miserable pirate. There are other roosters around." But they didn't have lanky legs.

The train arrived in Vienna. Red couldn't see much of a difference. She was in some kind of marshaling yard with loading docks that looked like missing teeth. She got off the train with Georgie's MPs. A Chrysler was waiting for her with a lot of little flags on its roof. She got into the car. Red was all alone. She didn't even have a Russian escort. Her driver could have been a male doughnut dolly. He was wearing the same uniform as Red. He introduced himself.

"Corporal Joey Mars. At your service, Lieutenant, ma'am."

"Are you my guide?"

"Sort of, ma'am. I'm a political compromise. The whole goddamn power structure is afraid of you."

"Why?"

"You have the Old Man's ear."

"But this is Vienna, Joe."

"Makes no difference, ma'am. The Third Army is sitting right over the hill. And Patton loves to roll."

"And you think the general would start a war over me?"

"I have my orders, ma'am. I can't afford to think."

"Corporal Mars, you're an imbecile."

"Exactly, ma'am. That's why the four-power commission chose a kid from the Red Cross."

"Well, you can stuff yourself, Joe. I want to see the blue Danube. And then I want a Sacher torte."

"The Danube isn't blue, ma'am. Not in Vienna."

"Of course it's blue. Everybody knows that. Would Strauss have written his waltzes if the Danube wasn't blue? Drive," she said.

They stopped at a little gray canal. "This can't be the Danube." The Hornet wouldn't have bothered to pee in a river like that.

"I'm discouraged, Joe. I kidnapped a train. Do you know how expensive that is? And the Danube doesn't even exist. I will start a war if I can't have my Sacher torte."

They passed an enormous cathedral with a crippled dome. It had turned black from all the bombings. She saw mountains of rubble, and next to one of the mountains was the Hotel Sacher, with a ragged red awning and wounds in its front wall.

The corporal accompanied Margaret into the hotel. She was greeted by doormen in rumpled pants. The Sacher had its own coffeehouse, half of which was closed; the other half was cluttered with generals who sat with gorgeous girls. The generals all stood up when Red appeared with Corporal Mars. Even the fräuleins saluted her. A table had been reserved for them near the window.

"Sacher torte," she said to the waiter. "Two. And two coffees with milk."

"Excellent," the waiter said, scribbling in an enormous pad.

Two slivers of thin, flat chocolate cake arrived with the coffee. Margaret was almost delirious after the first bite. She'd developed a habit for Hershey bars. But that prick of a major was right. The Sacher torte was out of this or any other world. It was very, very light. Not like a Yankee Doodle, which always stuck to the roof of your mouth.

But something troubled Margaret. None of the other generals and their fräuleins were eating Sacher tortes.

"Corporal Mars, are we lepers, or what?"

"No, ma'am. The Sacher only had enough ingredients to make one Sacher torte . . . for you, ma'am. There are counterfeit cakes. You can find Sacher tortes at the other hotels. But not at the Hotel Sacher. What we're having is the real thing."

"Fine," she said. "Good. Now I'd like to go to the Lipizzaner stables."

"The stables were bombed, ma'am. There are no Lipizzaners in Vienna. They're tucked away in the American zone."

"Naturally. But I was hoping we could find a couple of stray stallions."

"Not a chance."

She returned to the marshaling yard, kissed the corporal good-bye, and rode out of a blackened city that had lost its Lipizzaners and its own blue Danube.

ROLAND

11

• I listened to Red. I wasn't trying to bleed information about her love affair with the Old Man, or whatever you called it. But I had to know about George, about his nights and days after the war, when he moved to Bad Tölz, and the whole Third Army had become a band of military policemen. He had his own palace on a lake. Were there dances every night? I didn't ask. Did Bones McHenry ever appear with his sax?

George wasn't cut out to be a policeman. He should have seized Berlin when he had the chance. Then the war would have had a different ending, with the Russkies sucking on dead roots. He had all this dynamite, the Third Army. Hell on Wheels.

He and Red and Willie would go for rides in the Bavarian Alps. He'd rescued the Lipizzaners. Patton himself had become the Lipizzaners' "ward."

"Red," I asked with a jealousy I couldn't control, "did you ride a Lipizzaner?"

"Once."

I cursed myself for asking, as I imagined her on Hirohito's horse.

"Did you bring that horse to the Alps?"

"No, silly. We had picnics in the general's Cadillac. . . . He was drinking a lot, wasting away."

"But he had you."

"Shut up, Roland. I was a doughnut girl, not his companion or his concubine. He could just as well have died when they took the Third Army away from him."

"But he had America. He had Willie, his fame, his wife, his daughters . . . grandchildren. Christ," I said, "he could have run General Motors."

"He had nothing. . . . He was a warrior without a war."

He danced, he bowled with the Red Cross girls. He gave out penicillin to his soldiers, saved them from the clap. He wanted to kill Russians, not get involved in a denazification program.

"I couldn't help him, Roland. None of the girls could. . . . He was an antique the day the war ended."

"And you?"

"I'd still be delivering doughnuts if the army had let him keep his command. It was the sadness that killed him . . . not a car crash. I bumped into Mario somewhere. It could have been Rome. I can't remember."

"And you decided to live with him."

"Did it make a difference? He was writing a novel . . . about George. And I figured, good, I'll have my own encyclopedia of the Third Army. Besides, Mario was always nuts about me."

"Encyclopedia," I said. "He didn't roll with us. He sat on his fat ass, drinking the cognac I got from the krauts."

"Paint yourself a pretty picture, Captain Kidd. You stole behind Georgie's back. . . . Forget about Mario. He isn't worth one hair off a Lipizzaner's back."

But we couldn't forget. Mario appeared like a ghost at Karp & Co., in the book department. The son of a bitch had finished his novel. It was a main selection of the Book of the Month. Mario had written a roman à clef called *The Green Hornet*. He took our history, banalized us and the ETO. I appeared in the book as Captain Kidd, a snot-nosed officer who raided German warehouses as his own personal hobby. I'd surrounded myself with colored gangsters, MPs who murdered at my command. I'd seduced a redhead from Missouri, hypnotized Patton's dog, turned the mutt into an accomplice. Mario claimed that William the Conqueror was a cowardly dog, that the first sign of a bombardment sent him running for his life, and the pup wouldn't come out from under Georgie's bed.

I'd served with Willie, had never seen him grovel in the midst of fire. He sat like a sergeant major in the general's jeep, helped us capture all those Hungarians . . .

There was a book party at Brentano's. I arrived with Red, who carried a wicker basket under one arm. The place was packed. I barely recognized Mario. The fat man had grown thin in Chicago. He wore a simple corduroy suit, like a soldier-novelist who'd come home from war country to mythologize tank battalions and the quicksilver thrusts of the Green Hornet. A hundred people stood on line for Mario's autograph. He wouldn't even nod to us. We'd become waifs who'd walked out of his own book. We weren't bankable in

Brentano's, only nuisances he'd have liked to get rid of.

"Yes," I heard him brag to a dowager who grabbed up several signed copies of *The Green Hornet.* "I saw the general every day. He briefed me in his tent. He took me into battle, without his dog. Willie wouldn't leave the tent."

The pup lived in every war zone. He wouldn't desert the Old Man. I'd seen him wear goggles like a tanker. But you couldn't find that in Mario's book, only dilettante pirates, fallen freckle-faces, and cowardly dogs.

We approached the table where Mario sat with his dwindling tower of books. The line had already deepened behind us. There didn't seem to be enough of Mario's books at Brentano's. He charmed his admirers with his gaunt smile. "I loved George. He was a great man."

Finally, it was our turn. I had nothing to tell Mario. He was neither a novelist nor a soldier, but a man who rummaged through graveyards to rob the raw bones of history.

He flinched as Red began to recite from his book.

" 'The general wasn't even looking for a dog. But he had nothing to do one day and wandered through a London kennel. It was love at first sight. *Lemme have the pup,* he said, and brought a bull terrier back to his mansion at Peover Hall. The dog had belonged to an RAF pilot, who took him on nineteen bombing missions over Berlin. Patton named the pup William the Conqueror. But this William had no courage at all.' "

The novelist smiled. "Thank you, Red. But I'm familiar with my prose. You don't have to fling it at me. I'll stick to what I said. Willie was a coward and a pest."

Margaret opened her wicker basket. The pup jumped onto the table, overturned the tower of books.

Mario trembled. "I won't be manhandled. I won't be manhandled. Bring in the Board of Health," he shouted at Brentano's manager. "You can't have dogs in a bookstore."

"Apologize," Red told Mario.

"To whom? To what? That's not Patton's dog."

Red reached back and socked Mario in the face. He fell off his chair, slid against a shelf, and a wall of books tumbled down on him.

Margaret was arrested. I couldn't do a thing. Retailers didn't mean much in a bookstore. The dog was impounded, whisked away to a police kennel. I glared at Mario, wished I had a killer's instinct, like the little general. Mario washed his face in Brentano's sink and went on signing books.

I visited Red at the women's house of detention. She didn't complain. "I'm glad I punched him. I'd do it again."

I'd already put Dad on the case. He had his lawyer sit down with Mario. The man must have been made of silk. He stroked the novelist, had him drop the charges against Willie and Red. We had to go all the way out to Queens to locate Willie, who sat in a cage with dogs who were beneath his dignity.

Mario continued to hound us. We couldn't get out from under his *Green Hornet.* People at Karp's demanded my autograph, looked at Willie and Red with fear and trembling, as if gods had come to sit in a department store.

Red wanted to leave. "I can't stand it, Roland."

I took her out of the basement, let her work in the design

department. Christian Dior had already dropped a bombshell over Paris. Macy's and Saks and Bendel's couldn't seem to get enough of the Dior look: women dressed like mannequins who'd never been through a war and could have stepped out of some wonderland, with their black gloves, pinched waists, and hats as long as battleships. We had no grand salon at Karp's, no elegant fitting rooms, no foreign couturiers. Our designers could only steal from Dior, do him the downtown way. Red had her own curious ambition. She hid out on the fourth floor, far from our customers, who didn't have to gape at "Scarlett O'Hara of the ETO." It hurt our romance. Red was always locked in with the designers, creating Karp's new look. Mom warmed to her suddenly, as she could read the revenue that was growing out of Red's designs.

I barely saw her twice a week. We'd go jumping at the Savoy, where the hunchback was still occupying the second bandstand. Mario's book had jolted her somehow. She wouldn't talk of her time with the Old Man at Bad Tölz, wouldn't talk of the Lipizzaners. I dreamed of those white horses. They'd waltz through my living room, or prance on the roof at Karp & Co., their hooves beating against my heart. They were no circus animals. These were aristocrats, like the Hornet himself. I never saw a rider on their backs. The Lipizzaners swayed like a ballet of breathing tanks.

12

• Had to happen. Lizabeth fell out of love. Was it my negligence toward little Jon, letting him crawl into the melancholy thunder of my own schemes? Or was it "Rollie's war mistress," as Mom liked to call Red. I suppose it was a little of everything. A husband who couldn't make a future with his own wife, who was hooked into the past like a drug addict, who danced at the Savoy with a doughnut girl and a dog.

We didn't quarrel, and Lizabeth wasn't the kind who'd skulk around with another man. She was divorcing me and marrying her banker, Tim Cave, a childhood friend. I moved into my office, camped out at Karp's. Now that I didn't have Lizabeth's largesse, I had to demand a salary from Mom. The president of a department store should have been making sixty grand. But mom haggled with me. It was her form of punishment.

"Fifty," she said.

"And a Christmas bonus."

"If we have a fabulous year."

I'd become the pariah, Captain Kidd, who couldn't even hold onto his wife.

"Spider," she said, "you're not even a man."

"Careful, Mom. I'm still president of Karp's."

"And I'm chairman of the board," she hissed with such hatred in her eyes, I had to look in the other direction.

"I'll give up half my visiting privileges. You can have more of Jon."

"I don't need your gratuities. I've arranged things with Lizabeth. . . . Call yourself a father. You have a stone in your heart."

Mom's ancestry was acting up. She was an aristocrat from Silesia, and I was half Saxon, tainted with my father's blood.

"My soldier boy," she said, "who served with an anti-Semite . . . Yes, I know how he liberated Buchenwald, and you weren't even there."

"I was sent home, Mom."

"In disgrace. Stealing from German warehouses. I read *The Green Hornet*."

"It's a novel, Mom, only a novel."

"But the author is accurate about Captain Kidd."

The princess had spoken. Why should I contradict her? What good would it have done?

Like the Roosevelts and the Morgenthaus, Mom had a house in the Hudson valley, her own estate—Wild Farms—which her parents had handed down to her; it was at Wild Farms that I'd spent my holidays as a kid. I hated it, the big rambling house with servants who occupied half a floor and were only visible when Mom wanted them to be. I'd fallen in love with the gardener's girl. Mimi was her name. She didn't have red hair, but she was voluptuous at fourteen, and

I craved her kindnesses, the aromas of her skin. Dad couldn't keep his eyes off her. She made the whole house dizzy with her particular musk. She polished furniture when she wasn't at school, and I would read to her, lend her books when we weren't playing strip poker in her room, with its tiny bureau and even tinier bed. And when I bought her a mirror with my own money, edged in gold, something to relieve that terrible starkness, Mom got rid of the gardener, and little Mimi had to go.

The goddamn mirror, that was my sin. I'd contradicted Mom's sense of Wild Farms, where a gardener's girl couldn't have a gilded mirror in her room. I raged at Mom, because she hadn't given me the chance to tell Mimi good-bye. I struck her with my fist. Mom's brothers, who were visiting Wild Farms, knocked me to the ground.

"I'll send him to boarding school . . . in Alaska," Mom said, rubbing her face.

Dad came in, and all the commotion died. I was under house arrest for a week, couldn't leave my room. But I wasn't a bit sorry that I'd socked her in the face. And Mom and I had a gilded mirror between us, though I never mentioned Mimi again. None of my other girlfriends could waken me, not even Lizabeth. I slumbered until I found Red in the ETO. They had little in common, a gardener's girl and a redheaded reader of books. But that's how love goes.

And fifteen years after Mom made Mimi permanently invisible, she broke her silence.

"You'll never forgive me. . . . I separated you from that hot little bitch."

"The gardener's girl?"

"She threw her sex around."

"Mom, she was fourteen."

"A tigress."

"Yeah. With the devil's own tail."

"Don't mock me. I'm your mother."

"Mock you, Madam Chairman? I wouldn't know how. I'm just a boy from Wild Farms."

"You went to Cornell. You saw the world. You were the aide of that anti-Semite."

"He won the war. We didn't have to capture any German generals. They surrendered to George."

"Grow up, Mr. President. You're not a captain anymore."

And Mom walked out of Karp & Co., wouldn't even say hello to my dog. I didn't feel like presidenting a department store. I had Dad's chauffeur drive me and Willie up to Wild Farms. I hadn't been there since '44, when I was a ninety-day wonder about to join Georgie in the ETO.

The servants didn't recognize me. They thought I was some trespasser with his own pup. I had to growl at them.

"Diana, Phil, make me lunch."

They looked at me. "Mr. Roland?"

And we embraced.

"It's so good to see you, sir. We have your picture in our scrapbook. You can't imagine how proud we are of you . . . our own little lord rushing into Germany with General Patton."

Their little lord. Mario had been right about me. I *was* a

snot-nosed kid, born with a silver spoon up his ass, the brat who could visit Hyde Park with Uncle Henry Morgenthau and smoke a cigarette with the president of the United States.

I called him Mr. Frank. He liked to play poker. Uncle Henry would wink at me. You had to let the president win. "Grand," he would say, after I dealt him a royal flush. I was great at card tricks. How did I get assigned to the Third Army? By presidential decree. Mr. Frank adored the Green Hornet. They were both aristocrats. And he gave me to George.

But I didn't want to strut in front of Diana and Phil, who'd practically raised me during my long weekends at Wild Farms. I visited the room where I'd slept. It was about as big as an army barrack. I went onto my terrace, looked at the Hudson, but I couldn't fish out a single memory. I crossed over to the servants' side of the house. Now I was the trespasser. I entered Mimi's old room. The furniture had never been changed. Her little bed and battered bureau could summon up her smells with a brutal quickness.

I stayed at Wild Farms, did all my business on the telephone. A week went by. I talked to Red. She was all excited about her latest designs. I didn't ask her out to Wild Farms.

"Roland, I want to go dancing. When are you coming home?"

"Soon," I said.

I lingered, walked in the woods with William the Conqueror, who was frightened of chipmunks. I didn't mind. I knew he'd bark if there were Nazis around.

I stayed on and on. It wasn't Mom or Dad who rescued me. Lizabeth came up to Wild Farms. She didn't bring her banker, or mention the details of our divorce.

"I wish I could keep loving you, Roland, but I can't. You'll always be a captain in some army. I wouldn't mind bivouacking with you for the rest of my life. But you wouldn't ever let Jon or me into your tent."

"I'm sorry, Lizabeth. The war made me wild."

She laughed. "You were always wild. That's what I liked about you. Rollie, you can't camp here. Not in your mother's house. You'll only wither away."

She was right, of course.

I rode back to Manhattan with Lizabeth, William the Conqueror on my knee.

"You don't have to live in a department store, Rollie. You could stay with us for a little while."

"You have a new husband in the house."

"Tim and I aren't married yet."

She parked her big Hudson across from Karp's, wouldn't cry in front of Captain Kidd. "I can't cure you, darling. You have a son. See him sometime."

I entered the department store with William the Conqueror. My employees stared at us as if we were moon creatures. I went up to the fifth floor. Mom sat behind my desk. She'd summoned all the designers at Karp's. A cigarette dangled from her mouth . . . and Red's. I didn't like the complicity between them, felt estranged from their language. Mom didn't even acknowledge me or my dog. And Red smoked her cigarette, drank a shot of whiskey with the other designers, clutching the little glass like a magic thimble. She was already drunk.

"We'll steal from Dior," she said, like one of Mom's confidential pirates. "Anna, we'll flood the basement with that high-society look."

"We'll bankrupt Macy's," Mom said. "And Bendel's."

They both had blood in their eyes.

"We'll create an aristocracy for the masses," Mom continued. "Let Dior sue us. We don't need a license from him."

"Anna, we'll license ourselves."

"Exactly."

"And call attention to Karp's, Madam Chairman," I shouted. "Have lawyers and union reps visit our basement. We'll be ruined in a week."

"What's he babbling about?" Mom asked, with whiskey on her tongue.

"Karp & Co. thrives in the shadows. Do your Dior, but not in my basement."

"Do we have a choice, Captain Kidd? You've lost your Harlem connection. Our basement is half-empty. Or haven't you looked? Oh, I forgot. You were on a pilgrimage to Wild Farms. Did you notice that I haven't touched the decor in your room?"

"Mom, get the hell out of my chair."

"Roland," Red managed to mutter as she wobbled around. "Don't talk to Anna like that."

The other designers sneaked out of my office. They didn't want to gamble where the real power lay. With Mom or Captain Kidd.

I shoved Mom out from behind my desk, while Red kicked at me and scratched my face. I wouldn't hit Red. I took the blows. But I tossed the two of them out of my office, locked the door, while William the Conqueror lay deep under my desk. I didn't scold him. He understood cannons, but not the fury of human beings outside the ETO. I waited until closing time, then marched downstairs to our bargain basement. The shelves and barrels had only a few dead items, junk that nobody could want. The liveliest bargain basement in America had become a mourner's palace. Willie growled at all the ghosts. The Green Hornet's pup had turned into an attack dog again.

13

• I ran uptown to Booker Bell. Sergeant Muldoon sat among Booker's gang in a silver wheelchair, laughing and whistling to himself when he'd mutilated our men. He was paralyzed. One of Romulus' bullets had shattered his spine.

"What's the Milkman doing here? I thought Romulus hated him. . . . Don't you, Rom?"

The little general was silent all of a sudden.

"Niggers can't afford to hate," Booker said.

"That's the luxury of white people, I suppose. . . . What happened to my basement, Bookie? It's dry as a bone."

"We had to bring the Milkman in. As a consultant. We can't talk to the Brotherhood all alone."

"Which Brotherhood is that?"

"There's only one," Muldoon said. "The Brotherhood of Teamsters."

"Well, aren't we the Brotherhood of George?"

"We're children in a swamp compared to the Teamsters. Our trucks belong to them, our drivers. I told you, little man. We could supply one basement, not two. Manhasset's what killed us. The Brotherhood started paying attention to our war. . . . Now we don't have a single truck, and we're all on the blacklist. That means we're dead . . . and I don't want my son dying before his time."

"Can't we fight them?"

Booker started to laugh. "The Milkman kidnapped your son. What did he do? Fed him lollipops, sat him on his lap. The Brotherhood burns people alive–babies, grandmas, black or white. They only have one season. Success. If we war with them, they'll come into Harlem, eat the population."

"Then what the hell can I do?"

"Meet with the Man. Robinson Welles. He won't talk with us, but he'll talk with you."

"He's the Man? Then the Brotherhood is color-blind. Robinson's dad is black."

"The Brotherhood can afford to be color-blind with their own chief counsel."

Welles had served with General MacArthur, liberated Luzon. The Japanese called him the "gray gaijin," because he wasn't like MacArthur's other white ghosts. He had green eyes, a Roman nose, and coffee-colored skin. He was on the fencing team at Harvard. He joined a Jewish firm, Sandler & Son. The old WASP law firms wouldn't represent labor unions. That was the territory of Sandler & Son. Racketeers and labor leaders. And the Brotherhood's New York locals were Sandler's biggest client.

I'd met Robinson at different charity balls. He would dance with Lizabeth, a bachelor of forty who could have had his pick of brides. The "gray gaijin" had his own Harlem headquarters, where he would spend his afternoons with black politicians and the lame, the poor, the blind. The mayor cozened up to him. Robinson waved his hand, and a hospital was built. He lived on Riverside Drive, at the edge of Harlem, and he was chief counsel to locals that didn't have one black officer.

"I won't bargain with him."

Bookie grabbed me by the collar. "You'll bargain, little man. You'll bargain. . . ."

I phoned Sandler & Son. The firm was in the flower district, far from Wall Street and Madison Avenue. I didn't see Sandler or his son, unless they occupied a rear office. There was only Robinson and a couple of law clerks. His office wasn't large. I couldn't find any photos of Robinson with the president of the Teamsters. I couldn't find one diploma on the wall. It scared me. Robinson Welles didn't need a public mask.

"Rob," I said, without really greeting him. "Your general killed my general. He wouldn't let George near the Pacific after the Germans surrendered. It broke the Green Hornet's heart."

"What would Mac have done with the Third Army? You weren't jungle fighters. The Japs were sitting in caves. We had to get them out of there with torches, not a Sherman tank."

"George would have adjusted," I said, "but your man was a prima donna with a corncob pipe."

"And Patton? He'd have brought Willie along."

"So what?"

"That dog would have died of dysentery if the Japs didn't grab him first and roast him like a pig. . . . You had liebfraumilch. We didn't have a decent cup of water."

"You're jealous," I said. "Georgie inherited Hirohito's horse."

"Horse?"

"The Lipizzaner that Hitler had been saving for Hirohito."

Robinson rolled his green eyes. "We were starving, Rollie. We were inches away from eating human flesh. And you talk of Lipizzaners. Carnival horses."

"Schooled for emperors and kings."

"Maybe I like it better when horses can't go to school. . . . Booker Bell will have to work for us. You stole from Macy's and Gimbel's. You carted those goods on your trucks. You're a retailer. You know the rules. Anything with wheels on it is Teamster territory."

"And you'll burn us alive if we don't behave."

"Did I threaten you?" Robinson asked. "I talked to your mother yesterday, that dear woman. She gets more and more beautiful."

The son of a bitch had already negotiated with Mom. The Booker Bell Gang counted very little in his eyes.

"And the subject of your conversation?"

"Christian Dior."

"You're encouraging her to market phony Diors in my basement?"

"Absolutely . . . I want the boy, the trigger you have. Romulus Rivers Bell. He shot the Milkman."

"He's not for sale."

"You swiped him from the krauts."

"He's not for sale," I said. "He's a kid. I'm sending him to college."

144

"He set his last school on fire. He's part of Booker's gang, and that gang belongs to me."

I smiled at Robinson Welles, looked into his green eyes. "I'm also part of that gang. Who do I have to kill?"

He raised his hand to slap me. But I wouldn't have taken his slap. I'd dreamt of Lipizzaners. I'd rolled with George. There hadn't been any Teamsters in George's tanks.

"You'll run the store."

"As a puppet president."

"Come on, Rollie. We're not ghouls. We won't tamper with your people or your books. But we'll be your supplier."

"And what happens to Bookie?"

"He'll be my military policeman, like he was for Patton. Harlem has a whole network of illegal truckers. He'll keep those truckers in line."

"Turn them into a black local."

"The Brotherhood has enough black locals. . . . But don't cry. I'm bringing a touch of class to your business. I'll supervise the Diors. I told your mom which tailors to hire."

I started to shiver. He'd be in the store, work with Red. She'd fall in love with his green eyes. How could she resist a cultivated gangster? He wore the smartest clothes, neckties with a knot as crisp as a diamond, shoes with stippled marks. I'd have to kill the son of a bitch with the Green Hornet's gun.

We shook hands. I left the flower district, walked to Karp & Co., locked myself in with Willie. I wasn't like the Hornet. I had no strategies, no plans of attack.

Willie started eating my shoe.

145

14

• Booker might have broken heads for the Brotherhood, but he wouldn't sell his own son. He still believed Rom's gangsterism was a temporary gig. He couldn't afford such blindness around the Teamsters and Robinson Welles. There wasn't even a warning. The gray ghost sat in his office at Sandler & Son, while other ghosts, gray and white, marched into the Hotel Theresa without wearing a single mask and tossed Bookie out the window. That should have been the end of the Booker Bell Gang. But Robinson had never been around the Green Hornet, or been the mascot of a German officers' brothel. Rom resurrected the gang and declared war on the Brotherhood. He couldn't even give his own dad a decent burial. He was on the run. The new Romulus Rivers Bell Gang had one advantage: Harlem's tricky terrain. Robinson's ghosts could raid the Theresa, but they couldn't set fire to Sugar Hill without starting a civil war. They organized more black locals, hired black gunmen; Romulus Rivers Bell always got away. He was much more of a ghost than Robinson Welles.

I was the monkey in the middle. Had to do business with

the Brotherhood, but I didn't want Rom to die. Whatever uneasiness I felt about him, he was my second son. And I had my own war with Robinson. He'd destroyed the best MP I'd ever had. I wouldn't have survived the ETO without Booker Bell. I wanted to feed money to Rom, but I couldn't find him. And then Rom found me. He didn't have the remnants of Booker's gang with him, my lost MPs. He had a man with a missing ear and a murderer's blue eyes.

"Dad, meet the major."

I understood immediately: this major had been the commandant of Castle Höllenhund, had taught Rom how to kill.

"I smuggled him out of Munich. He was selling pencils in the street. You can call him Willy."

"Hello," said Major Willy.

"The kid worked for you, didn't he? He was your scout and your whore at Höllenhund."

"Dad," Rom said, "don't insult Willy. He's the love of my life."

"I'll bet."

"Ah, Captain Kidd. We're in a different war zone. I work for Romulus now."

"As his bodyguard-assassin?"

"Willy's my technical adviser. He says we have to capitulate."

"That's swell. And dance with your father's murderers?"

"Captain," Willy said, "we'll avenge Mr. Booker when the time is ripe."

"Once you join the Brotherhood, you'll have to wear the devil's tail."

Willie laughed. "I've worn it on many occasions."

"And what will you do? Walk up to Robinson with your hands in the air and say, 'I surrender'? He'll never believe you. He knows what the kid is capable of."

"But that's where you come in. You'll convince Mr. Robinson Welles. You'll tell him that you've reasoned with Mr. Romulus. That the Brotherhood will have to pay an indemnity to the Romulus Rivers Gang. Not cash. But a gift in Booker's name, something to remember him by."

"Like what?"

"That's the job of the convincer. You."

No Third Army man would ever have thought like that. Only the commandant of Höllenhund could have been so devious. But the son of a bitch was right. And I smiled to myself as I remembered the Green Hornet. What an army he could have built, with the major at his side. Stalin wouldn't have had a chance.

I smuggled those two assassins into Mom's sixtieth birthday bash. Anna was giving a party for herself in *my* basement at Karp & Co. She'd cleared out all the debris, and Red, her chief clothing designer, had turned Karp's into a cabaret. Red was Mom's magician. She'd reconstructed the Savoy, complete with its soda fountain and collapsible bandstand. And she was able to borrow one of the Savoy's biggest combos, Harry and his Hepcats. Harry had an exclusive contract with the Savoy. He wasn't supposed to play at private parties. And then I realized how Red had bagged the Hepcats. Through Anna's little ally, Robinson Welles. The bosses at the Savoy couldn't mess with the Brotherhood if they wanted to have their ice cream and tablecloths delivered.

I had to hide my fury. The Savoy was *our* club; Harry the Cat had witnessed my own love for Red. It was like a sacrilege seeing him and his trombone in this second Savoy. I couldn't scold Red (I'd have ruined Mom's soiree). And when I heard Harry wail, I realized I had lost her. She was dancing with Robinson Welles. He wore a tux that was much more elegant than mine. I had my old mothballed blue, with a rumpled tie. Rob was laughing right into Red's eyes.

Lizabeth had come with baby Jon and her banker husband, Tim Cave. Jon had grown into a giant. He must have been thriving with his new stepdad. I could barely recognize him as my own little boy. He'd adopted Tim Cave's strut, looked like a potential banker. Tim was doing business with my dad, might have bought into Karp's. I couldn't seem to dislike him. He was kind to Lizabeth. And he didn't condescend to Captain Kidd.

We shook hands like a pair of lumberjacks. Lizabeth kissed me on the mouth. Jon clutched my sleeve. "Roland," he said, "you haven't shaved properly. You have hairs on your chin."

Lizabeth shouted at him. "Jonathan, you mustn't say that to your father."

I was amazed at his sentences. He had Mozart's muscular music.

"Jon," I said, "you don't look into the mirror much when you live alone."

"But we invite you and invite you," Lizabeth said, "and you won't come for lunch."

"I'm too busy."

"It's Anna who runs the store . . . with her little accomplice." She caught me grinning like a lunatic, and she stopped. "We'll wait."

"Wait for what?" asked my giant of a son.

"Until the busy season ends."

I didn't even have to give any good-byes. Anna grabbed me away from my former wife. The Hepcats had prepared a slow number for the birthday queen, and I danced with Mom, while Willie bit my cuffs.

"Roland," she said, "did you have to bring that mongrel? He smells."

"He's General Patton's dog."

"But it's my party. And I didn't see Patton's dog on my invitation list."

"Should I leave with him, Anna?"

"You would. Walk out on your own mother's birthday."

Dad bumped into me with all the cachet of a man who'd been investing money all his life. "Son, I'll kill you if you make Anna cry."

"Allen, dear," Mom said, "calm yourself. I'll handle Roland." And she led me and Willie deeper into the dance. She was beautiful, I have to admit, a Silesian girl, without the steadiness of Dad's Saxon blood. Anna was capable of anything.

I abandoned her in the middle of that slow boogie, walked up to Robinson Welles, tapped him on the shoulder.

He wasn't pleased. And I couldn't get a smile out of his dancing partner. Red shoved Willie when he tried to dig his nose under her gown.

"Rob, we have business to discuss."

"Another time."

I could feel his bones shiver under the tux. He was crazy about Red. But she was a goddamn riddle. She'd drifted away from Captain Kidd. I couldn't bring her back into my orbit. All her passion had gone into those fake Christian Diors. Robinson wasn't even a rival. Red had become the princess of a department store.

"Now," I said, and Robinson Welles bowed to my own distant darling. "Be back in a minute, babe."

I brought him to the soda fountain, and the two assassins suddenly appeared. Romulus Rivers Bell and Captain Willy. Robinson blinked once and never lost the malicious romance of his smile. "Roland, did you set me up at Anna's birthday party?"

"The kid doesn't want to fight anymore."

"And who's the muscle?"

"Him? Major Willy. The kid's prime minister."

"That's cute. Is he named after Patton's dog?"

"No, Rob. It's a fucking coincidence, an accident of war."

"I don't believe in accidents."

"Come on. We'll all have a Golden Goose."

But Mom's soda jerk had never been near the Savoy, knew none of its habits. I had to step behind the counter and improvise. I stirred caramel-candy dust into a bottle of milk, chopped up a few mint-chocolate wafers and coffee beans, broke open a brick of vanilla ice cream, stuffed that cocktail into a malted machine, and served it in Coca-Cola glasses. We all started to drink—the major, Rom, Rob, and me. The Golden Goose worked like honey on Robinson Welles. He had much less menace in his mulatto eyes.

"Let me hear it from the kid."

"I can't beat the Brotherhood," Rom said.

"I sentenced Bookie to death. That was my call."

"It wasn't personal," Rom said, with just the right quiver on his lip. "Besides, I have another dad. Captain Kidd."

"And you don't hate me?" Robinson said, sipping from his Goose.

"I hate you. But I'm a businessman, a politician . . . like Robinson Welles."

"And you'd kill me if you had the chance."

"I would, but let's hope that chance never comes."

I was still the monkey in the middle. "Rob," I said, "you'll have to make a little restitution."

"How? Cash to the kid?"

"No. The Brotherhood will set up a scholarship, the Booker Bell Fund, for colored students . . . help them go to Harvard."

"It's a deal," Robinson said, and we clinked our Coca-Cola glasses. I should have brimmed with a pirate's joy. But I watched that Major Willy, and I watched Red watching him. My heart behaved like a sick rubber band. I'd been the fool, frightened that Robinson would grab my girl. She was only interested in an SS-man, with little nicks near his eyes, dueling scars he must have got from Heidelberg, or some other kraut college. I wanted to dig at his face with my Coca-Cola glass, but I couldn't attack the kid's prime minister. I'd have queered the deal. How had Red fallen in love with the commandant of Höllenhund? I should never have come home from the war.

Harry the Cat stopped wailing, sank deeper into the cellar with his band. Where was Bones McHenry? Red hadn't bothered to steal him from the Savoy. A white saxophone player with a hump on his back. I wished for Bones. I waited and waited, but Bones didn't come.

RED

15

● *Christian Dior.*

Margaret could have crossed the ocean, run to the Avenue Montaigne, sat at the master's feet, and studied all his mannequins, but she preferred to steal from him. "War is dead," the master had declared. "I don't want my models looking like commandos. I want blue umbrellas and black velvet gloves, skirts that wrap a leg with all the complication of a flower." The master had started Dior New York, licensed his designs, lent a few of his models to Seventh Avenue showrooms. But Margaret couldn't compete with Seventh Avenue, or Saks and Bendel's. If the master dubbed his latest line "Zig Zag," "Cyclone," or "Oblique," Margaret offered her own little cyclone in the basement at Karp's, without mannequins or ads in *Harper's Bazaar*. It was simple word of mouth.

Stylish women came to Karp's. They didn't need millionaire husbands or fat bank accounts. They could afford Karp's café-society look. And for Margaret it was the revenge of a doughnut dolly, as if she were setting on fire the uniform she wore in the ETO, finding another skin. She had to forget George, and that moribund army at Bad Tölz.

She went to The Baroness with Anna Karp. It was a private club for wealthy women merchants. Anna was proud of Red, liked to show her off. "My freckle-face, Margaret Young. She designs for me."

They'd enter in skirts and hats from Karp's spring line, looking like aristocratic mannequins. The whole clientele at The Baroness fell madly in love with Margaret. They wanted to hire her away from Anna, give her seed money to start her own collection. But Red was much too shrewd for these ladies. She couldn't have survived without the womb of a bargain basement. And what did seed money mean to her? She'd never had a job until she came to Karp's. She'd gone from doughnuts to a department store, with a couple of lost years in between.

"Imagine," Anna would brag at The Baroness. "I started out hating Red. She broke up my son's marriage. But now I'm glad. The two of us are finished with Roland, aren't we, dear?"

And what could Red say? It saddened her to be around Rollie. She'd start thinking of the Hornet, and what might have been. She felt like a war orphan with Willie and Captain Kidd. And she was rolling along, with the sudden thrill of a career . . . until she saw that phantom at Anna's birthday party, Müller the Magnificent, and she was sucked right back into the war.

She vanished from the party, but he followed her into the street.

"What are you playing this time?" she asked, practically

spitting in his face. "Farnsworth, Bruce? Or a rocket scientist?"

"I'm with the Romulus Rivers Gang."

"My God," she said, "you belong to that homicidal brat?"

"He was my pupil at Castle Höllenhund."

"Your love slave, you mean. Rollie says he was a murderer and a whore."

"Rollie could be wrong."

"Well, darling, do you have the same sharp spoon? Will you cut my throat in America?"

He kissed her, held Margaret close, and her heart beat like a maddened bird. She shoved him away, got into a cab, but the major's mark was already on her. She thought of hiring someone to have him killed. She might have asked Robinson Welles for a favor. But she couldn't involve Rob. He was sending her flowers, courting Margaret. He was a handsome devil, and she couldn't have had a fall and spring line without him and the Brotherhood, but he didn't arouse much passion in Red. He was like a general who'd never been near the ETO. He kept courting Margaret.

"We could go to the Bahamas, babe."

"On a short honeymoon, huh?"

"Make it as long as you want."

"But I already have a man," she said, not sure if she was lying or not.

"Who? Captain Kidd? You haven't been near him in months. I've checked it out."

"Have you been spying on me, Rob?"

"Night and day."

And Red was almost charmed by the brutal frankness of the Brotherhood's little king. He was trembling, and she could feel the pain of his devotion to her. She might have been moved at another time. But her life had suddenly turned upside down. She didn't belong to Robinson Welles or Captain Kidd. And now she had to wonder if she belonged to that kissing bandit, Major Willy.

Rob would have bumped him off if he'd found Willy and her together, and she'd have been like a jilted bride without her Christian Diors. But the Romulus Rivers Gang was clever enough. That baby gangster himself arranged the rendezvous. There was murder in his eyes. He was in love with the major, but he had to protect him from Robinson Welles. He was sixteen years old, the best union organizer the Brotherhood had ever had. He destroyed maverick locals, tracked down renegade truckers, obliged them to join the Brotherhood. But he had Willy to guide him now. Willy was his mentor.

A truck would arrive in front of Karp & Co. without a single mark. She would be summoned downstairs. Romulus Rivers Bell would wave to her from the cab. The back door would open. She'd close her eyes, get scooped off her feet, and land inside the truck, which was both a boudoir *and* a heart of darkness, with candles, a bed, and bottles of champagne. And she couldn't deny that she loved the intrigue of it all. The major had reconstructed his own Höllenhund. They couldn't go to restaurants, or to a film. The Brotherhood had a whole world of tattletales.

And so she had Major Willy all to herself inside a curious

tunnel, with Rom at the wheel of a mobile love nest. He'd drive, park, order caviar and champagne. Occasionally, he would eat with them. He rarely said a word. The major would command him to speak, but it was Rom's gang. Rom was the general.

"Romulus," she'd ask, "would you rather I met Willy somewhere else?"

And suddenly he'd start to speak. "Mademoiselle, there is nowhere else. Robinson would find you. And I'd have to arrange the funeral."

The boy was eaten up with jealousy. But he couldn't menace Margaret without risking the major's wrath. He was caught inside a pickle jar. He had to drive the truck. And Margaret had idyllic afternoons away from Karp & Co. Anna spotted her absences. She didn't scold.

"You're in love with that awful Nazi, aren't you, child?"

"I suppose I am."

"And what if it all explodes in our face? I see how Robinson looks at you. He's worse than Othello . . . totally obsessed."

"I could always leave. I wouldn't want to harm the store."

"Don't be ridiculous. We couldn't survive without you. We wouldn't have a winter line. And you're like my own daughter. Roland is lost to me."

"Anna, don't say that."

"It's true. He's my enemy. He had a sweetheart once. A little peasant who worked for us. I fired her. And Roland can't forgive me. He's malicious. Didn't he let his own general down?"

"It was an accident."

"He was almost court-martialed. And then he hires the man who ruins him. Mr. Powder Burns Monroe. Puts him in my store."

"Rollie was right. Monroe is the best security man in town."

"Child, be careful. I'm not worrying about the store. I'm worried about you."

They kissed, an ex–doughnut dolly and a Silesian princess. But she had to jeopardize Karp's. She'd work like a demon in the morning, designing Christian Diors, have lunch with Robinson, or go to The Baroness with Anna Karp, and lend herself to the Romulus Rivers Gang in the late afternoon, live inside a truck that was much darker than the doughnut wagon she'd had to drive for George.

She'd ask Willy about his dueling scars.

"It's nothing. We had secret societies. It was another age. Not like America. We thought of ourselves as aristocrats. And that was the sign. Coming as close as possible to having one of your eyes plucked out. But I prefer it here."

"Did you really rescue Mussolini?"

"Ah, that old chestnut. It's a lie. I wasn't aboard one of the glider planes that landed on Mussolini's mountain. I didn't grab him away from his captors. I had a broken leg. But I helped plan the operation. Freckles, it was a brilliant surprise. We wanted to capture Churchill the same way."

"And George Patton."

His scars crinkled in the dark. "That was my biggest failure. We weren't scared of Eisenhower. We had better chiefs.

Hitler was insane, but he couldn't rule us from his bunker in Berlin. We would have captured your general . . . if Captain Kidd hadn't stumbled onto Höllenhund."

"Then he's an unsung hero of the war."

"No. The little Gypsy betrayed us."

"Rom?"

"I had Roland in my sights. I'd prepared the trap. One minute more . . . but the idiot had never seen such an odd group of warriors. A colored MP, a dog, and a tall, skinny captain. He was distracted. And he changed sides. I'd taught him too well. He must have known in an instant that America was his real fatherland. I wanted to kill him. But he was right."

They'd drink champagne, kiss, rock with the truck's slow motion, and Margaret would finger the scars on the major's body. He could have been a medieval knight. And when they'd lie in each other's arms, it was almost like betraying the Green Hornet, even if she hadn't slept with George. Roland wasn't on her mind. Roland had become Robinson Crusoe, with his own Man Friday, the general's dog, who shouldn't have been upstairs in an office at Karp & Co. The dog was as fake as Red's Christian Diors. He looked like Willie, nuzzled her like Willie, but somehow he wasn't the same dog. And here she was, sleeping in a truck with the very man who'd tried to kill the Hornet. She was shameless, and she deserved whatever hell the commandant of Höllenhund could bring her.

That hell came quite soon, though it wasn't entirely the major's fault. Rob and his Brotherhood had chosen the first winner of the Booker Bell Fund Award, with a full scholarship to Harvard College. He held the ceremonies at one of his Harlem locals. Romulus had to attend. The scholarship was in his father's name. He brought the major with him, as if he were laughing into the teeth of Robinson Welles. And Rob brought Anna and Red. Even Captain Kidd had come, in rolled-up pants, to salute Booker's memory. The local was packed. Rob stood on the dais, without a microphone. He wore dark wool, with a silk handkerchief and Spanish boots. His green eyes burned in the local's dimmed lights. Red watched a couple of women swoon. She wasn't in love with Rob. He was a little too magnificent. But she'd misjudged him. He was as much of a strategist as the Green Hornet.

"Ladies and gentlemen, we're here to celebrate a remarkable soldier. Sergeant Booker Bell, a colored man who fought in Patton's Third Army, who rolled across the Rhine with him, proving once and for all that when it comes to battle, there is no color line. He was our associate before he died. . . ."

"Before you dropped him out the window," Margaret muttered to herself.

"And I cannot allow his death to remain unnoticed. And so we've established a fund in his honor to help a deserving colored student attend Harvard College. But there's a catch, ladies and gentlemen. We'd only be dishonoring Booker if we didn't honor his adopted son. More than anything in the world, Booker wanted a genuine education for Romulus Rivers Bell, a boy whom Booker rescued from a slave labor camp and brought to America, where he grew up in Harlem with his dad. Romulus Rivers Bell is the Brotherhood's chief troubleshooter. We're all indebted to him. But I tried to grant his father's wish. What can I tell you? I pulled some strings. I'm a Harvard man, and I persuaded the college to accept Romulus Rivers Bell as a special student in the fall, when he'll live and work among Harvard's freshman class. And so the Brotherhood awards the first Booker Bell scholarship to Mr. Romulus Rivers Bell. . . ."

Rom was brooding in his seat. He grasped all the mischief behind Robinson's selection of him. He wouldn't move until the major whispered in his ear. Then he walked up to the dais, shook Robinson's hand, and accepted the scholarship. But he couldn't bring himself to thank the Brotherhood.

It didn't matter. In one diabolical stroke, Rob had separated Rom and the major, diminished their little gang, and canceled Red's love life. Who would dare drive the "honeymoon" truck after Rom was gone?

16

• Red had a slight reprieve. The special student didn't have to appear in Harvard Yard until the middle of next month. She had most of August and some of September to ride around with the commandant. She'd already missed her period. And she didn't need a doctor's divining rod to notify her that she was pregnant. Willy flooded her with champagne, but Rom wasn't so jubilant.

"*Junge*," Willy said, "can't you share the happiest day in my life?"

"Is that why you're sending me to Harvard? So you can be with her and whatever's baking in her belly?"

The major reached out to strike Rom. But he couldn't. "Rom, that louse has us boxed in. How could you throw back at Rob a scholarship in your father's name?"

"I'm not a colored kid."

"You are," the major said, "philosophically speaking. Weren't you in a labor camp?"

"And who put me in there?"

"But if you hadn't gone to Höllenhund, we might have never met. . . . Freckles, appeal to him."

"I can't. I'm not a referee."

"Harvard," the major said, "is almost as good as Heidelberg."

Romulus smiled. "Will I have dueling scars to show for my experience?"

"This is America. Dueling was outlawed ages ago. But you'll mingle with the sons of corporation presidents."

"Willy, I'd rather mingle with you."

"You'll have your vacations. Meanwhile, take care of Freckles. Christ, we still have a month."

"I can't enjoy it. I keep counting off the days."

Margaret was like him. She drank the champagne, kissed the major's scars, spent long afternoons in the truck, but there was a touch of hysteria to everything she did. Robinson Welles would win.

Her belly grew. She went with Rom to Brooks Brothers, picked the charcoal colors he would have to wear if he wanted to thrive at Harvard.

"I look like an undertaker," he said.

"Sonny, that's sort of the idea. Nothing conspicuous. You have to blend in."

"Like your Christian Diors."

"It's not the same galaxy," she said. "Or would you prefer to wear skirts?"

"Freckles, I wore them all the time at Höllenhund. I was the major's bitch. He liked me in skirts. A lot of officers did."

She didn't know whether to weep for him or scratch his eyes out.

"Maybe Harvard's another Höllenhund. I'll give you all

the skirts you want. You can model them in your dormitory. But pack the charcoal suits. Just in case."

And she hugged her rival, Romulus Rivers Bell. She rode with him and Willy to Penn Station, sat him in the right car, with his luggage and his ticket. She hated Rob. He'd sentenced Rom to a slow kind of death. How would the boy fit in? Whoring couldn't have prepared him for a college curriculum. He'd end up on probation, like a convict, have to return to Harlem and the Theresa Hotel.

He clutched Red's hand. "Write me every day."

She got off the train with Willy. They climbed the marble steps. And there he was, at the top of the stairs, with a raincoat wrapped around him like a bat's wings. Robinson Welles.

"It's heartwarming," he said. "Rom's two comrades seeing him off. I was a little late."

Robinson had no cadres behind him, no hitmen from the Brotherhood. But there was an ice storm in his eyes that could have swallowed Penn Station.

"Rob," she said, "aren't you going to invite us to lunch?"

They went to Lüchow's, sat at the king's table, reserved for the Brotherhood and all its guests. The three of them drank chilled white wine, that liebfraumilch Rollie had loved to steal. Robinson wasn't impolite. He didn't talk business at the table, mention the Christian Diors that had turned Karp's basement into a monumental success. He talked mostly about Robinson Welles.

"I grew up on Sugar Hill. My dad was a light-skinned nigger from Panama. Mom was a Rockette. Dad took her right out of the chorus line. He was an irresistible man, a swindler who traveled around the country selling insurance policies that couldn't bring you back a dime. He borrowed, he stole, but none of his creditors could ever find Mr. Welles. Dad was invisible once he returned to darktown and all the black gentry of Sugar Hill. He hired tutors for me. Colored college professors. I inherited Mom's looks and Dad's finesse. I marched into the Dalton School for Boys, took their entrance exam, wrote about trickery in Shakespeare. The teachers were stunned."

Margaret swirled liebfraumilch in her mouth.

"They groomed me for Harvard. Had my interview with a pair of lawyer alums. I didn't hide my nigger blood. I romanced them with tales of Sugar Hill, how Dutch Schultz's Harlem connection was our next-door neighbor. . . ."

People kept coming up to Rob. They'd curtsy and whisper in his ear. The waiter would bring him a telephone. He'd pick up the receiver, listen, and say, "No, no, no, down the line . . . and don't bother me. I'm in the middle of a meeting."

But he couldn't continue. After the tenth or eleventh man curtsied to him, Rob got up from the table. "Sorry, but I have to settle a feud at one of our locals. . . . Finish your lunch. And don't bother about the bill. It's on the Brotherhood."

Red waited until Robinson Welles walked out of Lüchow's; then she grabbed Willy's sleeve. "Darling, you'll have to leave town. Tonight."

"Don't be silly."

"Isn't it clear what all his jabber was about? He was marking time while he plotted your destruction."

Willy was adamant. He wouldn't run.

No gunmen arrived at the table. But where could she go with Willy? They skulked downstairs to Lüchow's labyrinthian rest rooms, and made love in a telephone booth, like a pair of desperate children.

Willy survived September and October. He collected bills for the Brotherhood. But no matter how ingenious he was in finding phantom telephone booths, Red couldn't disguise her own fears. It was like hugging a doomed man.

And then Rom returned from Harvard for a weekend, visited her designing room at Karp's. She was astonished. Romulus had remade himself in a month and a half. He wore a crimson turtleneck with "Harvard" across his chest. He talked of Kant and Diderot, the power of Tolstoy's prose. He was like a Wellesley girl. He did offer to drive the "honeymoon" truck. But there were no more honeymoons for Red. She was in her fifth month. She had to refashion Christian Dior to disguise her pregnancy. Robinson Welles wasn't a fool. She was full in the face, very plump. He'd stare at her, his green eyes saddened by her subterfuge. But he welcomed Rom. "We're all proud."

"I could break heads in the Boston area. Just ask."

"Aren't you ashamed? The Brotherhood's only scholar preaching acts of violence."

"But it's in my philosophy book. Nietzsche said that a little blood could go a long way."

Robinson laughed. "I'll die. They're raising anarchists at my old college."

And he ducked his head into his limousine, disappeared from Karp & Co., while Willy grabbed Rom's turtleneck and started to strangle him in the middle of the street.

"*Junge,* who was your first professor?"

"You, Herr Major."

"And didn't I tell you that philosophers were like thieves, hiding behind a mask of words?"

"*Ja, ja,*" the boy said, with tears in his eyes, and the major let go of his Harvard turtleneck. "But I have to believe in something. I'm my own father's fellow."

"You're my bitch."

"Willy, you have it wrong. She's your bitch. Mademoiselle Freckles."

Rom returned to Harvard, rumpled and forlorn. Red couldn't comfort him. He'd crept outside the universe of Karp & Co. And Willy was helpless without the umbilical cord of a proper gang. He was hit by a truck while collecting money in the garment district. It was slaughter on Seventh Avenue, arranged by Robinson Welles.

Margaret didn't even have to hear about it. The baby jumped in her belly, and she knew that the major was dead. She wouldn't attend the grotesque funeral that the Brotherhood provided for one of its fallen heroes. Romulus was also absent. And Robinson Welles, the Brotherhood's chief counsel in the East, must have assumed that Rom had buried himself in some graveyard of books. Rom was his badge of safety. No Harvard man would ever mistreat another. He was wrong. Rom arrived at the law offices of Sandler & Son in his crimson turtleneck and clawed Rob, kicked his teeth in, just like he would have done to the Brotherhood's most dangerous competitors. Willy had taught him those tricks at Höllenhund.

Six or seven law clerks had seen Romulus come in and out, heard Robinson's moans, and called the police. But Romulus didn't go back to his dorm or attend another class. He vanished from the streets. Red had to mourn him *and* Willy. She wouldn't mourn Robinson Welles, who lay dying at Bellevue, while his henchmen hunted the Harvard boy. Rob wanted to see Red. She wouldn't go, but Anna pleaded with her. "Child, we can't exist without the Brotherhood. Forget your feelings . . . for my sake."

She couldn't forget. But she walked to Bellevue in a dark veil and a darker dress. Robinson was surrounded by his bodyguards. He had a tube in his nose. His face was purple from the beating Romulus had delivered. He wore bandages on his head that looked like a skullcap. She almost pitied him.

"You shouldn't have had the major killed."

He had to whisper. "I'd kill any man who came near you. . . . You're carrying his child."

"But I didn't encourage you. I didn't lead you on. I'm not in love with you, Rob. I never was."

He coughed, and whispered again. "No matter, Red. All your suitors would have come to the same consequence. It's called search-and-destroy. . . . You would have ended up in a lonely circle."

"Like you," she said.

"Babe, will you kiss a man before he dies?"

But Red couldn't kiss him. He started coughing blood.

Nurses screamed at her. She left the hospital. But she paid a price. She couldn't produce Christian Diors without the Brotherhood's protection. The basement emptied out within a month.

The Silesian princess, Anna Karp, began to pull out her hair. She couldn't show up at a posh restaurant or a private club with a pregnant bachelorette like Margaret Young. But she still adored Margaret. Margaret wasn't like that ungrateful son who sat in his office near the roof with a smelly dog and wouldn't lift a finger for Karp's. Anna had to fire half her employees. She wouldn't fire Red. It was Red who decided to quit.

"You could stay," Anna said

"A designer with nothing to design. I'll become a hermit. Like Captain Kidd."

"Don't mention him. The Karps will take care of you. The baby . . . I'll have a second grandchild."

"Anna, I can't stay."

"Then you'll draw six months' salary. I insist."

"A bonus, Anna, when the store is like a haunted galleon?"

"Six months. I insist."

They hugged, and Red walked out into the November wind.

ROLAND

17

• I watched it all. Mom's dismantling of the troops, Major Willy's departure into another world. I was no goddamn Greek chorus, adding my own two bits to the action. I only ventured downstairs after Mom abandoned the store. Karp's had no money in the bank. Our bookkeeper came to the last nominal exec. Captain Kidd.

"Sidney," I said, "do the payroll."

"How, Mr. Kahn? I could go to jail."

"I'll countersign all the checks. It's my responsibility."

"Then you could go to jail, sir."

"I'll risk it. And stop calling me 'sir.' Didn't you bring me toys when I was a baby? You were at Karp's before I was born. How many payrolls have we ever missed?"

"None, Mr. Kahn."

"And we won't miss one now."

I had to investigate the damage, look into our inventory. We had no inventory. Clerks stood behind counters with nothing to sell. We had a few bibelots. That was it.

I rode up to Harlem and the Theresa Hotel, looked for the Milkman, Sergeant Muldoon, someone who'd rolled with

George. But the Milkman couldn't advertise himself. He'd been too close to that kid who'd crippled him, put him in a wheelchair. And the Brotherhood might have taken its revenge on Muldoon. I wandered about in the lobby, and a shoeshine boy slipped a note into my hand. I couldn't tell whose scrawl it was, but I examined the note.

George Raft and Betty Grable. Suite 806.

I smiled at the Green Hornet's passwords: *Raft* and *Grable.* I knocked on the door of 806, went in. The Milkman was sitting in the dark with a shotgun across his lap.

"You came for cash, didn't you, Captain Kidd?"

"Couldn't we shake up Harlem, steal a little?"

"Harlem's already shook up. The Brotherhood has seventy hitters on the street with one thing on their mind. Romulus Rivers Bell. I could lend you sixty dollars."

"Thanks, Muldoon, but I have to pay a department store."

"The Brotherhood wants you out of business, Captain. Abandon ship."

I made an appointment with my ex-wife. How could Lizabeth refuse me? All she had to do was write one little check. Her hubby, Tim Cave, was there when I arrived, and it lent a kind of sting to my visit. Couldn't even talk to her in private. Lizabeth needed her own chancellor around me.

"We're sinking," I said. "I can't meet my payroll."

Lizabeth looked at me. "You don't call. You don't write. You haven't even asked about Jon."

"Is he ill?"

"He's marvelous. His vocabulary grows and grows. He's starting to scribble. He keeps writing about you. *Poor Roland.* That's what he calls his dad."

"Can I see him?"

"He's at nursery school right now. And I can't give you a check, Roland."

"It's the Brotherhood," Tim said. "They've threatened to damage Jon if Lizabeth goes near you and the department store."

"Is the Brotherhood like an octopus? Does it have a million tentacles? *They* threatened Lizabeth? Who's this *they*?"

"Robinson Welles."

"But he's dead."

"Roland, he was live enough to telephone me."

"From Bellevue?"

"I didn't ask. He said, quote: 'Good morning, Tim. Regards to the wife. If she offers a penny to that scumbag, Captain Kidd, some little boy will be in serious trouble. Good-bye.' "

"I'll strangle him."

"Roland, you can't win. Sell the store. Give it away."

I returned to Karp's. I had my Jewish bookkeeper prepare the payroll. I had a week before the checks would bounce.

"It's unethical, Mr. Kahn."

"So what? Anything can happen. God could rescue us."

"You shouldn't speak of Him like that. The Lord isn't a gambler."

But we didn't have to close our doors. Customers would wander in from time to time, grab something away from our dwindling stock, and leave our shelves a little more barren. I waited. None of my checks bounced. I expected the city marshals to come with their trucks and collect whatever valuables Karp & Co. still had on its floor. There were no marshals or men to summon me to court. I strolled the store with Willie, like some demented warrior, and refused to fire another clerk.

"You'll see," my bookkeeper said. "The cops will arrest us both. I've already prepared a little suitcase."

We had other visitors. Burly truckers who arrived with a man in their arms. The guy had a green face. It was Robinson Welles, wrapped in a hospital blanket, wearing a tweed cap. He couldn't forget about fashion, no matter how near he was to death. He signaled to me with his little finger, and his truckers carried him up to my office and locked the door.

"You bailed me out, didn't you, Rob?"

"I sang a little song to your bank, moved my own savings into Karp's account."

"Why? You pulled away the Brotherhood's protection. You could have brought me out for peanuts."

"Rollie, it's not my ambition to run a department store. Look at me. I'm all twisted."

"It could have been worse."

Robinson started to cough. "How much worse? That kid broke my face and bent my body into a pretzel."

"But you're not dead, Rob, and there has to be a reason. Romulus gave you the gift of life."

"Gift?"

"He's a killing machine. He could have snuffed you in a second. But he didn't. He wanted you to survive."

"So I can look back at the monster in the mirror?"

"Maybe. You took out Major Willy."

"The major's my business. He was romancing Red behind my back. He knocked her up. He had to go."

"But if you'd rolled with us, Rob, instead of mucking around with General MacArthur in the Philippines, you'd have realized that Romulus was the major's whore."

"The major was romancing Romulus *and* Red?"

"Probably not. But Rom was still in love with that SS-man."

"Hell," Robinson said. "It doesn't give him the right to attack his own employer."

"You didn't toss his dad out the window?"

"Shut your trap. You belong to me, Captain Kidd."

"And what happens now?"

"I'm your personal Santa. I smother you with merchandise. But you stick to the store. You don't look for Rom. You don't look for Red."

"And if I refuse?"

"Then you and your mutt won't make it to the new year."

And he left my office in the truckers' arms, General MacArthur's green-eyed ghost.

18

• We rose right out of the ruins, had a sensational Christmas. We captured the December market, competed with Macy's and Gimbel's. I never asked where the goods came from. I closed my eyes and trucks would appear. Robinson Welles was navigating Karp & Co. from his hospital bed. I had to rehire the troops Mom had fired. Even Powder Burns Monroe, who had bolted during our financial crisis, came begging for his old job. I didn't punish Georgie's G-2. But I put him under the Milkman. I'd brought Sergeant Muldoon down from the Theresa Hotel, made him my second in command. He'd roam Karp's in his silver wheelchair, listen to customers' complaints, coaching the sixteen Santa Clauses we'd distributed throughout Karp & Co.

Lawyers from Christian Dior arrived with a ton of briefs. They were prepared to sue us into the ground. I served them whiskey in my office. "Gentlemen, see for yourselves. We're a gigantic bargain basement. We can't afford a spring line."

"Sir," the chief negotiator said, "we can track pirated coats and dresses to this department store."

"Then there must have been a cabal inside Karp's that was strictly illegal."

"Do I have your word that this pirating will stop?"

"More than my word."

He handed me a copy of Mario English's novel. "We idolize *The Green Hornet.* Will you sign it for us, Mr. Kahn?"

"I'm not the author."

"But you are Captain Kidd, and this, I believe, is General Patton's dog."

I wanted to cut out their hearts, but I couldn't. Had to play a character in the novel, or they might have continued their suit. I stroked Willie, but he wasn't interested in lawyers who represented Christian Dior. I signed that copy of the *Green Hornet* near Mario's name, and we parted on pleasant terms. But something gnawed at Captain Kidd. Romulus' *mercy* toward Robinson Welles. What could the kid have gained by letting Robinson himself lead the manhunt against him?

I knew the kid was in Harlem somewhere. That was the one home he'd ever had in the United States, outside Harvard Yard, and he couldn't attend any classes in Kierkegaard or Kant with a legion of hunters on his tail. And how could I walk Harlem, when Rob had his own walkers everywhere? I had to think of what might tempt Rom, bring him out into the open. Books. I drifted into that tiny paradise of second-hand bookshops on Fourth Avenue. I hung around the philosophy sections, patient as a spider. I couldn't understand a word of Kant. The kid had outgrown me. I discovered obscure philosophers who talked about America as the leviathan that had to feed itself on more and more products. I welcomed this leviathan, or Karp's might have gone out of business.

I'd become so enchanted with reading, I forgot to look up. It was the kid who shoved me out of my reverie, Romulus Rivers Bell, who stood beside me in a Fourth Avenue cave, wearing his Harvard turtleneck. One of the sleeves had already unraveled. And I had my own terrible intuition, like a flash Kant himself might have had.

"It was no accident. You wanted him alive."

"Dad," the kid said. "Can't you say hello?"

"You couldn't resist . . . philosophy books."

"You're wrong, Dad. You thought I couldn't resist. That's why you came to Fourth Avenue. I can read you like the bumps on my palm."

I started to shiver. This savage boy, who could have had me killed on the road to Höllenhund if he'd decided to raise his hand, felt more like family than my own mom and dad.

"Little schemer," I said, "you've had your taste of Harvard, and you're hooked. You expect me to convince Robinson to let you keep your fellowship, after you manhandled him."

"Dad, he murdered Bookie and the major. He had to pay."

"But you decided on the price."

"That's how you bargain. With your fists. . . . I'm hopeless without Kierkegaard."

I couldn't abandon him. His whole damn identity was

locked inside a crimson sweater. The Loreleis must have left their embankment on the Rhine and crossed the ocean like good little mermaids and landed on a rock in the River Charles. Not even Loreleis could resist the call of Harvard Yard. They'd seduced a little Gypsy with their American songs.

I brought the kid to Lüchow's, asked for the Brotherhood's table. Rom swallowed half a bread and a dish of noodles.

"Stop it. Your stomach will burst." But he went on eating . . . until Robinson arrived in the arms of his truckers, wearing the same blanket and tweed cap.

"Rob, what took you so long? The kid's eating himself into the grave."

"You had to bring him here, huh?"

"Where else could I bring him? The whole city's one big mousetrap."

"My chef's on route from Brotherhood Hall. He'll carve you both into a turkey in front of all the guests."

"Shame," I had to sing out. "Can the Brotherhood afford to lose its first Booker Bell scholar? You'd have to eat your own fellowship. A union that destroys its anointed ones."

"Shut up."

"Rob, think about your career. You know how reporters like to dig. What if you decided to make a run for the White House?"

He almost laughed. "A nigger president in the shape of a pretzel."

"A war hero," I said. "The gray ghost who plowed right

through the Japanese war machine . . . and is guilty of infanticide."

"This murderer at my table is an infant?"

"He's sixteen. You got him into Harvard. He's your protégé."

"He has to apologize, kiss my finger, or he doesn't leave Lüchow's alive."

But Rob was no match for a kid in a crimson sweater. "Boss, I'd do it all over again."

Robinson rocked in his blanket. "Rollie, you're my witness. I gave him a second chance."

"The kid is reckless, but he's also right. You harmed his loved ones. He had to react. He's your angel of mercy, Rob."

"Shut up."

"If you were the kid, you would have done the same thing."

Rom was gulping his noodles.

"Get him out of my sight."

"A full pardon. No mysterious strangers creeping into his dormitory with hammers in their fists."

"Out," said Robinson Welles.

Romulus finished the noodles and wiped his mouth. "Good-bye, Dad."

"He doesn't return to Manhattan until he graduates. Is that understood?"

"And you'll fix it with the dean for all the days he's missed?"

"He's with the Brotherhood. I don't have to fix a thing."

"Good-bye, Dad." The kid was crying now.

I couldn't help myself. I hugged him like a soldier son going off to battle.

He marched out of the restaurant in his ragged clothes.

"Great," Rob muttered. "I lost my appetite with him around. Where's Red?"

"Wish I knew."

"Where's Red?"

19

• Sixteen Santa Clauses.

We had to hire a dozen more. Shoppers descended upon Union Square, and I wondered if we'd have an avalanche, if Karp's would cave in from so many customers. There was a fever in Manhattan, a hysterical urge to buy and buy before 1950 jumped into our face. I wasn't so eager for 1950. I didn't want the decade to end. The decade belonged to us, those pale warriors of Patton's Third Army. We had little to do with Mario English and his novel. It was a lot of crap. I tried to escape *The Green Hornet.* But shoppers would come upstairs from our book department, ask for Willie and me. I couldn't bark at them. I couldn't growl. I was a retailer, a merchant. I had to perform, play Captain Kidd, with Willie at my heels.

I'd run up to the Savoy as often as I could, praying that if I shut my eyes, Red would appear at the soda fountain, sucking on a Golden Goose. She had to be in her seventh month, and there was a load of vitamins in a Savoy milk shake. Robinson Welles wanted to kill her for messing around with the major and carrying his child. I didn't want to kill Red. I'd lost her somewhere between the ETO and a

188

department store. And now I had a platoon of Santa Clauses and no Red.

All I could find at the Savoy was that white hunchback, Bones McHenry, and his sax. He was still the Savoy's second-string band. And I didn't have Red to dance with while he tootled. I might have been dreaming, but I swear he was sending me messages with his sax. He stood behind his roped-off little mound and pointed his "golden goose" at men who had nothing to do but watch Bones McHenry and Captain Kidd. They weren't the Savoy's regular bouncers. They were bouncers from the Brotherhood, waiting to kidnap Red.

Harlem was closed to her. I realized that. I had the Milkman check all his sources. I even went to Powder Burns, whom I felt like strangling.

"Tell me how Red could vanish without a trace."

"Captain Kahn, she's a disappearer, that girl."

"But how did she manage it?"

"Luck, fate . . . a good accomplice."

"Mario English?"

"I doubt that she'd hook onto Mario, sir."

"Damn it, you're 'sirring' me again. You outranked me in the ETO, or did you forget?"

"Ex-colonels don't mean much in these times, Captain Kahn."

"*The Green Hornet* is still on top of the best-seller list."

"That's what I mean. It's fantasy. Another *Gone with the Wind.*"

I sent him back to his security detail. Anna arrived. She wanted to reclaim her designing rooms, do Balenciaga instead of Christian Dior. Not a chance. I'd already ripped out her designing boards, turned Karp's entire fashion department into an upstairs annex.

"You had no right," she said, "no right to massacre the heart and brains of the store."

"Heart and brains? We were bankrupt. You fired half of Karp's. . . . Mom, you can't come back."

"Darling," she said, "do you have the lawyers to fight me? You certainly don't have the shares."

"But I have the Brotherhood. Robinson Welles. We couldn't have stayed open without Rob. We're murdering Gimbel's. Should I tell him you're unhappy with the deal, that you'd like me to step down?"

"I raised a rattlesnake."

"It's nothing. All the Karps thrive on poisoned milk."

She slapped my face in front of a dozen employees. "It's the gardener's girl. You can't stop hating your own mother."

I wasn't thinking of little Mimi, and strip-poker games in her barren room at Wild Farms. I was thinking of Red.

"Mom, you can have your Balenciaga. But bring me Red."

She walked out of Karp's. I followed Mom to her votive restaurant, The Baroness, where males weren't really welcome.

"Roland, you're embarrassing me."

"Red," I grumbled, "Red."

"Imbecile, I haven't the slightest notion where that child is. She simply evaporated."

That's all I needed to know. Mom lied like a Silesian

princess, with all the studied ice of her upbringing. But Dad was the puritan, not Mom, who couldn't mask the explosive passion of the Karps.

I left the restaurant, returned to Union Square. It was the day after Christmas, but we couldn't let go of a single Santa Claus. We didn't have to mark down our prices, announce any sales. Customers kept coming. Our barrels couldn't stay empty when we had our own battalion: Robinson's trucks. Clerks clung to me. "Mr. Kahn, Mr. Kahn, we need credit approval."

I locked myself in with the Milkman.

"Sergeant, can you roll without me? I have to take a little trip. And you have to cover my flank. In case Robinson calls."

"What do I tell him, Captain?"

"I'm busy signing books and collecting dollars for the Brotherhood. He can't have the least suspicion that I've left the shop."

"Boss, I'll say, 'It's the Christmas push. Captain's running around Karp's like a crazy chicken.' "

I knew the Brotherhood was following me. Rob had to figure that I'd lead him to Red. I grabbed Willie, shoved him into a shopping bag, and went out the front door wearing stuff from our bargain table, most of me hidden in a scarf half a mile long. I kept changing cabs until I arrived at the Bronx border. Then I had a limousine service drive me up the Hudson to Mom's estate. The servants didn't seem so eager to see Mr. Roland at Wild Farms. Phil had a .22 under his belt, and Diana was clutching a kitchen knife.

I smiled. Red was in the house. Red was in the house! And Diana and Phil were protecting her from intruders ... like Robinson Welles and Captain Kidd. Mom might have left Phil instructions to shoot me on sight. That was his privilege. I went into the house. The Hudson's own Lorelei must have been singing in my ear. I didn't have to scurry around. I hiked up to Mimi's old room, which Mom had refurbished for Red. She had one of Phil's rifles cradled on her belly.

"I'll shoot."

All I noticed was the raw brilliance of her freckles as the sun beat down on her face.

RED

20

• It could have been a fairy tale. She was in a haunted house, waiting for her frog prince. She knew Roland would leave his pirate's perch and come up the Hudson with that lamentable dog, who was as fake as Mario's novel. The frog prince had brown eyes. He couldn't dance or kiss like a dead major, but he'd always been her beau. She hated him. She couldn't forgive his nonchalance, selling caviar in the middle of war, just like a frog prince. And Margaret greeted him at Wild Farms with a rifle. She wouldn't talk to Rollie. He'd have to live inside her silences like some contortionist or fabled lindy dancer from the Savoy. But the dog would scratch at her door, and finally she came down for breakfast, clutching Shakespeare's sonnets, the rifle under one arm. Roland was at the breakfast table, with Diana and Phil, who served him pancakes. She disregarded the dog and Captain Kidd, mumbled Shakespeare to herself, the Shakespeare of her childhood, when she was a fireman's daughter in Minneapolis.

"You miss George, don't you, Red?"

"Nobody asked you to drop in your two cents."

The mutt tried to crawl under her maternity dress, and

she slapped him on the nose with Shakespeare's sonnets. He was mortified. His pink eyes went from panic to rage.

"Why did you bring this pretender?"

"Red, you're wrong. He dreams of George. I hear him every night. He misses the Old Man."

"I don't dream of you, Captain Kidd. I dream of the major. He didn't peddle liebfraumilch. I could shoot your eyes out."

She was crying while she sat there. "Damn you, Roland Kahn. George couldn't survive without you. The reporters would bait him, and he'd answer like a wild dog. You would have swept them away, gotten them and Eisenhower out of his hair."

"I loved you . . ."

"Then you wouldn't have worried so much about wine and caviar. But the gentleman officer from Cornell had to prove how good a pirate he was. . . . I fall into a fury each time I remember that this was the house you played in as a child."

"It's Anna's house. I was like a guest."

"Isn't it wonderful to think so? Rollie the hermit who rolled right through the war. . . . You abandoned your own little boy. I'll have my child in this house, and then I'll run away from you all."

"No!"

It was Anna Karp, who'd come to the haunted house in her sable coat. She was shivering under the fur. "You'll stay with us." And she turned on the frog prince. "You've put her in danger. I talked to Robinson. He isn't stupid. His bloodhounds will track you to Wild Farms. They'll eat you alive, and then they'll bring Margaret to the ogre in his hospital bed."

"We have rifles, Mom."

The telephone rang. It was the other frog prince, Robinson Welles, visiting through the wires. He asked for Margaret.

"Are you still in love with him, Red?"

She wouldn't answer.

"And I suppose he'd do the martyr's dance and get himself killed if my captains came for you."

She hung up on Robinson Welles. Anna pawed at her. "Is the ogre coming to Wild Farms?"

"Probably."

But Robinson Welles had his own idea of an army. Margaret didn't see bloodhounds, only a boy in a crimson turtleneck. He knocked on the door and entered.

"Christ," she said, "are you Rob's messenger?"

"Thanks to Captain Kidd. He patched things up. Robinson couldn't kill me without canceling my fellowship."

"Did you bring a knife and a gun?"

"No, Mademoiselle Freckles."

"Then how will you kidnap me?"

"I can't. Rob wants a hostage."

"Anna? I refuse."

"Freckles, Rob wouldn't touch a grandma. He likes Anna Karp."

"He can't have Roland," she said. "I'm not bargaining today."

"He doesn't want Roland," the boy said. "He wants the pup."

"Has he lost his mind in that hospital of his? What can a dog do for him?"

"Rob's a thinker, a Harvard man. And he figures you wouldn't stray too far without General Patton's dog."

She had to pinch herself to keep from laughing in the boy's face. He seemed so serious in his crimson colors. "This isn't Patton's dog. It's some other Willie. Rob knows that."

"But you're still attached to him, mademoiselle. He has some sentimental value. And Robinson is counting on that."

"What if the dog doesn't want to go with you?"

"Dad will have to convince him. Otherwise, you'll have blood on the carpets. His and mine."

She looked at Rollie, who was trembling. He grabbed the boy's turtleneck. "I negotiate like a demon, get you back into Harvard, and this is how you treat me?"

"Dad," the boy said, "we're all casualties. It's the bitter fruit of war."

"Assassin," Rollie said, "you've been trying to steal the general's dog ever since I laid eyes on you."

"Dad, this isn't the general's dog. . . . I'm trying to save your life."

"But he is the general's dog to me. That's all that matters."

"Dad . . ."

He'd lulled Margaret with his little lament. He twisted around on his heels, kicked Margaret's rifle across the room, hurled Diana and her kitchen knife to the floor, pulled the .22 out of Phil's pants, and aimed the gun at Roland, while Anna swooned into Phil's arms. Roland never flinched, and Margaret had a sudden surge of affection for her frog prince.

"Go on," he said. "Finish the job. But you're not taking Sergeant Willie."

The boy was lost. He didn't have Harvard or Höllenhund. He dropped Phil's .22 and ran out the door. Anna woke up, found herself in Phil's arms. "This is a lunatic asylum," she shouted. She hugged Red, put on her sable coat, and disappeared from Wild Farms.

Margaret went back to the room where Roland's little gardener's girl had once lived. Mimi. But other ghosts haunted that room above the Hudson. The Hornet appeared in front of her eyes. He didn't look like Julius Caesar or Alexander the Great. He had four stars and his Colt, but he wasn't really groomed the way he should have been. His boots weren't shined. His whipcord breeches had gaping holes. Her darling general looked like a bum. He must have come from Hades, or an American Höllenhund. She didn't even have a cigar to offer him. But she had plenty of blankets.

"General, are you cold?"

"All the time."

"Do you read newspapers where you are? Can you get your hands on the *New York Times*? You were right about the Russkies. They blockaded Berlin."

"Russkies," he said. "Russkies."

Margaret put a blanket around his shoulders, but the contact, the warmth of her hands, must have frightened this ghost, and he melted into the atmosphere like some kind of powerful vapor.

The days passed. She wouldn't go downstairs even when William the Conqueror invited Margaret to breakfast with scratches on her door. She would read her Shakespeare, recall the ancient young men at Buchenwald who loved Shakespeare's melodies more than the music of silver and gold. And then, on the last day of the year, she heard a familiar riff outside her door, a melodic line that seemed to wander out of her own past. The music called to her. How could Margaret resist? She marched downstairs with her rifle. Bones McHenry was in the living room with his big horn, playing for a pirate and a dog.

He winked at Margaret.

"Bones," she asked, "how did you get here?"

"Mr. Roland rented me."

"I don't understand. The Savoy would never release you, give up your services on the biggest night of the year."

"Heck," he said, "a white jazzman with a bump on his back? I'm a dime a dozen."

"Not at all," Roland interrupted. "The Savoy screamed blue murder. But I used Robinson's name."

Margaret was about to laugh. "Just like a pirate."

"Dance with me, Red. For auld lang syne. I'd like to celebrate all the doughnut girls, and hold onto nineteen-forty-nine."

"Go to hell."

But the sax must have softened her up. She grabbed Roland's neck, cupped in her belly, and she danced the Hudson River crawl.

"I'm dreaming of the major while I'm in your arms, Captain Kidd." She cried on Rollie's shoulder. ". . . I remember a beanpole in a captain's uniform who made love to me in a doughnut truck. He was engaged to an heiress, and he didn't lie about it."

"I wasn't that much poorer than Lizabeth."

"He's lying now."

"Only a little. Red, it wasn't the liebfraumilch. Topside would have found another reason to get rid of me. I was too close to George."

"Too close," she said, "and not close enough." The dog kept bumping between them. But not even William the Conqueror could halt their rhythm. Roland muttered *nineteen-forty-nine, nineteen-forty-nine.* He was holding onto the decade with all his might. And Margaret knew that as long as she hopped to Bones McHenry and his big horn, nothing could happen. . . . 1950 would never come.